HIDE AND DON'T SEEK

and other
very scary stories

ANICA MROSE RISSI

Illustrated by
CAROLINA GODINA

Quill Tree Books
An Imprint of HarperCollinsPublishers

Quill Tree Books is an imprint of HarperCollins Publishers.

Hide and Don't Seek

For information address HarperCollins Children's Books, a division of HarperCollins Publishers, 195 Broadway, New York, NY 10007.
www.harpercollinschildrens.com

Library of Congress Control Number: 2020949343
ISBN 978-0-06-302695-7

Typography by David DeWitt
21 22 23 24 25 PC/LSCH 10 9 8 7 6 5 4 3 2 1
❖
First Edition

For Ati. Boo!

CONTENTS

Dear Reader,

What scares you?

For me, the answer to that question changes often.

Sometimes I'm afraid of traditionally scary things—like monsters, ghosts, or mysterious sounds in the dark. I wake up at night in my comfortable bed and try *not* to think about what might hide beneath it.

Other times my fears are murkier. Their shapes are blurry and complex. Those kinds of fears are trickier to define—and harder to soothe or dismiss.

We tell spooky stories for many good reasons. Some are about the thrill of the scare. Some take the frightening and flip it until it's silly. Others poke hard at our deepest, darkest worries to prod out what's truly inside them. They make us imagine the worst coming true—and help us imagine surviving it.

They surprise us, amuse us, entertain us, and warn us. They horrify and delight us. They make us scream for more.

You'll find all types of scary stories in this collection. A few might make you laugh. A few might make you think. The spookiest will make you shiver.

If you're feeling brave, then turn the page. The first scare awaits you behind it.

—Anica Mrose Rissi

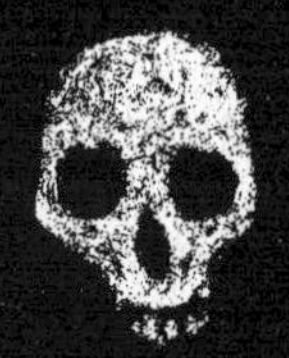

HIDE AND DON'T SEEK

Nikki wanted to play with her brother, Jeremiah. But Jeremiah wanted to play with his friends.

"Your friends aren't here yet," Nikki said. "Please, just one game before they come?"

Jeremiah gave in. "Okay. One game. You hide and I'll seek." He covered his eyes and counted out loud.

Nikki ran into the cornfield. She ran past rows and rows of corn, until she reached the edge of the field. She ducked between two round bales of hay that were almost taller than she was. She crouched and held as still as she could. She waited to be found.

But Jeremiah did not find her.

Nikki listened for her brother's footsteps, or for the two-note whistle—one high and one low—that would signal he'd given up and she'd won. She heard only the wind in the cornstalks.

It's a trick, she thought. *He's not coming.*

She sank to the ground. *He thinks he can just not play and get away with it. Well, I'll show him. I'm not moving until he finds me.* She leaned against a hay bale, and settled in for a nap.

When Nikki opened her eyes, the sun beat down from straight overhead. It was close to high noon. She must have slept for at least an hour. Nikki blinked and stretched. She reached for the sky, and heard a sound that made her freeze. It was her brother's whistle: one high note, one low. It sounded nearby.

Carefully, so he wouldn't hear her, Nikki peeked around the hay bales. The whistle came again: one high note, one low. Nikki pursed her lips to whistle the response—one low note, one high—to give Jeremiah a clue. But before she could blow, she spotted something strange: a man in a red plaid shirt.

The man turned toward Nikki, and she dropped down fast to her hiding spot. She held her breath, and waited for the man's approach. But he hadn't seen her. He retreated into the rows of corn.

Nikki's heart hammered her rib cage. Stranger Danger pulsed in her veins. She hoped Jeremiah would find her soon, before the unfamiliar man came back. She didn't dare whistle their signal or leave her hiding spot, in case the man was still there.

She would wait for her brother to rescue her. Once she saw him, she was certain she'd feel safe.

She waited.

And waited.

And waited, until she slept.

When Nikki opened her eyes, it was dusk. The wind in the corn was the only sound . . . until she heard it: Jeremiah's whistle. One high note, one low. Her chest filled with cautious hope.

Nikki peered around the hay bales, praying not to see the strange man. She didn't. But she didn't see her brother, either.

At first, Nikki saw no one. But the notes of the whistle sounded again, the leaves rustled, and an old man emerged from the rows of tall corn.

The man walked slowly, his back hunched over a cane. He seemed to be using the cane as much for sight as for balance. He felt his way past the large bales of hay, but did not see Nikki between them.

Nikki watched him retreat in the direction she longed to run—back through the cornfield, toward her house, where surely her brother and supper were waiting. But between here and there were likely two strangers. Nikki still didn't dare leave her hiding place.

Jeremiah will come soon. He'll bring the dogs. We'll all be safe, she assured herself.

She tried and tried to believe it. She hoped so hard, she wore herself out.

When Nikki woke up the third time, a full moon shone above. She heard the call of her brother's whistle, and almost mistook it for the wind. But the notes came again—one high, one low—and she knew it was finally him.

Nikki stepped out from between the hay bales, and jumped at what she saw. A pale, shimmering ghost wove in and out of the rows of corn. It was as bright and untouchable as moonlight, but as real as the terror that filled Nikki's lungs and drowned out her scream. The ghost floated away, and the whistle floated behind it. The sound jolted Nikki back to life.

She ran. She ran faster and harder than she'd ever run before—around the ghost, through the corn, over the hill, and toward home. She didn't look back to see if the ghost followed. She looked only forward, but her vision was blurred with tears. She saw nothing until she reached for the doorknob to her house, and saw it wasn't there.

Nikki gasped. The house was gone. The entire thing. Only a crumbled foundation was left in the place where her home had once been.

She wanted to sink to the ground, let the ghost and fear consume her. But she couldn't do that. She had to find Jeremiah.

She ran to the neighbor's house and banged on the door until, finally, someone answered.

Nikki had never seen the surprised-looking woman who opened the door in pajamas, but there was no time to ask who she was. The real question was much more important.

"Have you seen my brother?" Nikki asked. "Jeremiah?"

The woman appeared stunned. She blinked, then laughed. "Nice try, but I don't believe in ghosts." She tried to shut the door.

Nikki stopped her. "Ghosts?" she repeated.

"Jeremiah of the Cornfields, right?" the woman said. "The boy who lost his sister? The one who hides while he seeks?"

Nikki's mouth fell open. She found she couldn't speak.

The woman shook her head. "Sad story, if you believe it. Though at least the first part's true: The sister ran off to play hide-and-seek, and the boy couldn't find her. Thought she must have fallen asleep in the corn. But the search parties never found her, either, nor sign of her body or bones."

Nikki stared. The woman continued. "Their poor parents assumed she was kidnapped. The both of them died from grief. But the brother, Jeremiah, he never stopped looking. Every day of his life, he went out and searched. Called for the girl in the cornfields, but of course she never called back. He finally passed, a generation ago. Some say he's still there when the corn is tall, on nights when the moon is full. Whistling, whistling. But she never whistles back."

Nikki pinched herself, but she was fully awake. This wasn't a nightmare. It was real.

"What was her name?" she asked, to make sure. "The ghost's sister. The one who's missing."

The woman tilted her head to one side. "Well, gosh. I can't say. I guess if anyone knew, they've forgotten. She'd be long gone by now, that's for certain."

The woman smiled. "Oh, look. A pretty sunrise." She pointed behind Nikki.

Nikki turned and saw the orange sky. The

full moon was gone. Her heart felt empty.

"Go on home now," the woman said. She closed the door.

Nikki walked slowly to the cornfield. She moved through the corn grown high as her head, and skimmed its rough leaves with her fingers. She emerged on the side with the hay bales. She settled between them to wait.

BEATRICE

On Christmas morning, Beatrice ran downstairs and saw exactly what she was hoping to see: a gift too tall to fit under the Christmas tree. A gift that was, in fact, as tall as she was.

It was wrapped in silver paper and tied with a huge red bow. The card attached said *Love, Mom and Dad*. Beatrice clasped her hands together. "Is this what I think it is?" she asked.

Her father smiled into his eggnog. "Perhaps you should open it and find out," he said.

Beatrice untied the ribbon and removed the shiny paper, being very careful not to rip it. She had never been the type to tear open her presents. Unwrapping a gift slowly helped build the excitement.

Even though she'd known exactly what would be inside, Beatrice still gasped when she saw it: her very own life-size, walking, talking Looks Like Me Doll.

"She looks just like me!" Beatrice said.

The doll smiled Beatrice's smile. "That's the idea," the doll said.

"Oh, wow." Beatrice opened the clear plastic box, and the doll stepped out. "She sounds like me too."

"We sent in a recording of your voice," Beatrice's mother said. "And pictures, of course. Didn't they do a great job? The resemblance is uncanny."

Beatrice nodded. The doll nodded too. Beatrice giggled.

"Do you like it?" her father asked.

"I love her," Beatrice said. "Thank you so much. I think I'll call her Sunny."

"No," the doll said. "No, thank you."

Beatrice's parents laughed. "Preprogrammed with manners," her father said. "Very nice."

"You don't like the name Sunny? What name do you like instead?" Beatrice asked the doll.

"Beatrice," the doll said.

Beatrice frowned. "But I'm Beatrice."

"I'm Beatrice," the doll said. Beatrice's parents laughed again.

"The spitting image." Her father snapped a picture with his phone.

Beatrice shifted uncomfortably. She didn't want to upset the doll, but she also didn't want to share her name. But that was ridiculous—dolls didn't have feelings. Not even walking, talking look-alike dolls. "Maybe you could be

Beezy," she suggested.

The doll stared at her. Beatrice stared back. Beatrice blinked. The doll did not.

"Or we can figure your name out later," Beatrice said.

"Good idea," her father said. "Why don't you open your other presents?"

When all the gifts were unwrapped and she'd eaten her breakfast, Beatrice led the doll upstairs.

"This is my room. Our room," she told the doll. "I sleep up there." She pointed to the top bunk. "The bottom bunk can be yours."

The doll stared at the top bunk. She stared at the bottom bunk. She stared at Beatrice. She did not blink.

The doll walked to Beatrice's closet and opened the door. "Let's play dress-up," the doll said.

"Yes, let's!" Beatrice said. She loved dress-up. She'd always wished for a friend she could play it with.

"What's your favorite outfit?" the doll asked.

Beatrice showed her the red velvet dress she was planning to wear for Christmas dinner. "It's new," she said.

"Pretty," the doll said. She touched the lace collar. "May I try it?"

"Sure," Beatrice said.

The doll took off the leggings and polka-dot top she'd come with, and pulled on Beatrice's dress. Beatrice helped her zip it up in back, over the compartment where her batteries were kept. The dress fit the doll perfectly. She spun in a circle and the skirt billowed out. Beatrice was glad to see her so happy.

"Here," the doll said. She held out the outfit she'd just taken off. "You try these on."

"Okay," Beatrice said. She slid off her nightgown, pulled on the doll's clothes, and stood by her side in front of the full-length mirror. It was fun and a little weird, seeing herself in double.

"Who is the girl and who is the doll?" the doll said.

"I'm Beatrice," Beatrice said. "I'm the girl."

"I'm Beatrice," the doll said. "I'm the girl too."

Beatrice laughed. The doll was silly. "Let's do each other's hair," she said.

Beatrice untied the ribbons on the ends of the doll's braids, and loosened the locks into thick, dark waves. She was amazed how much it looked and felt like her own hair. She brushed the doll's hair and pinned back one side with her favorite barrette.

They turned to the mirror. "We really are twins," Beatrice said.

"Almost," the doll replied. The doll took the brush from Beatrice's hand. "Now I'll do yours," she said.

"Yes, please." Beatrice sat on the floor and

watched in the mirror as the doll brushed and parted her hair. The doll wove Beatrice's hair into two thick, dark braids. She tied the ends with the yellow ribbons that had been in her own hair.

Beatrice clapped, delighted. "I look just like you!" she said.

"And I look like you," the doll said.

"Who's the girl and who's the doll?" Beatrice asked their reflections.

"I'm Beatrice," the doll said.

"I'm Beatrice," Beatrice said. She grinned at the doll. The doll grinned back. "We still need a good name for you," Beatrice said. Beatrice blinked. The doll did not.

Beatrice startled at a knock on the door. "Come in," she said.

Beatrice's mother poked her head into the room. "Don't you look nice in that dress," she said. "Company will be arriving soon. Come downstairs and help me set the table?"

"Sure," Beatrice said.

"Sure," the doll said.

Beatrice's mother laughed. "I meant just you, Beatrice," she said to the doll. "The doll can stay here during Christmas dinner, I think."

"I'm Beatrice," Beatrice said. She climbed to her feet. "I'm the girl."

"No," the doll said. "I'm Beatrice. I'm the girl. You're the doll." She tossed her hair over her shoulder.

"That's not true!" Beatrice said. She looked to her mother for help.

Beatrice's mother shook her head. "Uncanny," she said, and laughed. The doll laughed too. Beatrice's heart raced.

Beatrice's mother stepped toward her. "Here," her mother said. "I think we can take its batteries out. That ought to stop the talking. You can put them back in later if you'd like."

Before Beatrice could protest, her mother

slipped a hand under the polka-dot top. Beatrice heard a soft *pop* and felt the strangest sensation in her back. She tried to speak, but no words came out.

"There," Beatrice's mother said. She dropped Beatrice's batteries into her pocket, and smiled at the doll. "All set, Beatrice?"

"Almost," the doll said. The doll scooped Beatrice up and placed her on the bottom bunk. Beatrice wanted to kick and scream, but she couldn't.

The doll pulled a soft blanket up to Beatrice's chin. Beatrice stared at the doll's face—her own face, really—as the doll tucked her in. Beatrice blinked. The doll did not.

The doll turned away from Beatrice, and took Beatrice's mother's hand. "All set," the doll said. "You know, I think I like her best when she's not talking."

Beatrice's mother shrugged. "Suit yourself. She's your doll."

The doll looked back over her shoulder and smiled. "See you later, Sunny," the doll said.

Beatrice blinked. She blinked and blinked a million times, desperate for her mother to notice.

"Bye, Sunny," Beatrice's mother said. "Merry Christmas."

The doll led Beatrice's mother out of the room, and pulled the door shut behind them.

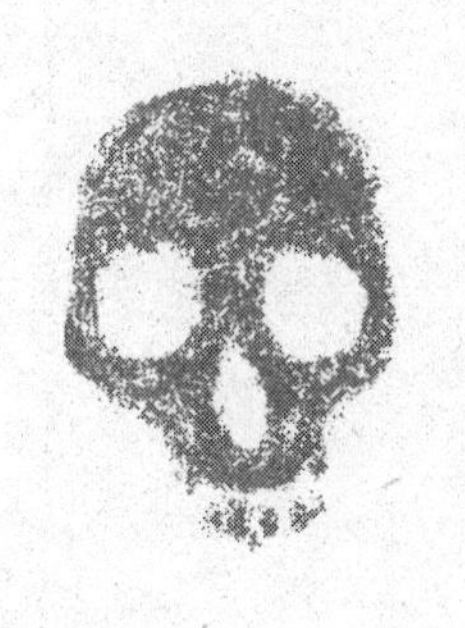

HAVE YOU HEARD

Have you heard the tale
of the scarecrow girl
who stands in the old witch's garden?

She holds her arms out
stiff from her sides,
aloft like they're almost forgotten.

But she'll never forget
for the pain is so deep.
How she wishes she could change position!

You can bet that the girl
now full well regrets
picking flowers without real permission.

YOU'RE IT

Hey

Hey

Who's this?

Your worst nightmare

Haha

No really

Sorry but it's true

OK

I guess I'm blocking you now

I'm afraid you can't do that

Why not?

Because:

Tag

You're it

Bye weirdo

I wouldn't do that if I were you

Do what?

Put down the phone

It won't work

You've been tagged

I'm sorry

I had to

Whatever game this is, I'm not playing

You're playing

And trust me, you can't afford to lose

You're really sick, you know that?

I'm not sick

I'm trapped

I got tagged

And it's your turn next

My turn to what

To pass it on

Before it's too late

Bug off

You can't scare me

Then why did you just close the curtains?

I didn't

Liar

You're peeking behind them

But you're looking in the wrong place

And for the wrong thing

GO AWAY

Moving to another room won't help

That's a nice kitchen, though

STOP WATCHING ME

I like that pic of you and your brother on the fridge

Is that your juice glass next to the sink?

Put the knife down

It can't help you

You won't find me

And you can't stop this

I'm sorry

I didn't want to believe in it either

What do you want

That's the wrong question

Tell me the right one

What does IT want?

Who's it?

You're it now

Remember?

IT got you

Don't let it stay

This isn't funny

I'm dead serious

You're it

And the clock is ticking

If you don't tag the next person, your time will run out

Forever

Tick tock

I'm turning off my phone now

No! Stop

You'll kill us both

What the

Why won't it turn off

What did you do

How are you doing this

I told you

I got tagged

Now you're tagged

We have no choice but to play

I quit

Believe me

I don't want to hurt you

But IT does

See?

OW

STOP

How did you do that

Why

You've got ten seconds left

To tag someone else

Choose a victim

Or you're done

Game over

Understand?

10

9

8

Stop!

7

6

I won't do it

5

I can't

4

3

2

* * *

Hey

Hi

I'm sorry

???

I'm so sorry

Who is this?

Your worst nightmare

TRULY DELICIOUS

Dear Dad and Nora,

How are you? I am great. Camp is good so far. The kids in my cabin are nice and so is our counselor, Alanya. The food is pretty bad, though, so if you feel like sending snacks, that would be awesome (hint, hint).

This morning I played tetherball with my bunkmate, Chloe. This afternoon I'll take the swim test.

Please pet Peanut for me and tell her I miss her.

Gotta go!

Love,

Robin

Dear Dad and Nora,

Thank you for the care package! The spray cheese is delicious and so are the crackers, but it's most fun to spray the cheese directly into my mouth. I'm glad to have something for days when lunch is gross.

Today they served us weird meat stew that smelled like boiled socks with the feet still in them. I only had an apple, but afterward Chloe and I ate the snacks you sent. We think maybe mosquitoes don't like spray cheese blood as much as they like foot-stew blood, because we got way fewer bites than most of our friends at campfire. Must be all those healthy chemicals they put in the can, haha.

Time for lights-out. Good night!

Love,

Robin

Dear Dad and Nora,

Today Chloe and I kayaked all the way around the lake. I have blisters on my palms from paddling. I thought we'd get to spy on fancy rich people's houses, but it turns out Camp Dunmore's the only place around here. Maybe fancy rich people are afraid of ginormous mosquitoes.

I don't blame them. The swarms are pretty bad. A bunch of kids from my cabin are covered in welts, and at night I hear them scratching. It makes me itchy, even though I don't have any bites. I am well protected by the power of spray cheese.

Speaking of which, please send more snacks! And kiss Peanut on the snout for me.

Love,

Robin

Dear Dad and Nora,

Quiet time is extra quiet today. A bunch of kids got sent to the infirmary, so they're not scratching in their bunks like usual. I said no wonder they got sick—they ate chunky swamp stew!—but Alanya says it's not food poisoning, it's bug bites. Plus exhaustion from heat and dehydration. One girl was so out of it, she fell over in the mess hall and took another camper down with her. Some people say she didn't fall, she lunged at him on purpose. I didn't see it, but whatever happened, the nurse took them to the infirmary to rest.

Chloe is fine, like me, and we're passing spray cheese back and forth between our bunks. Thanks for sending extra, and for all the bug spray too.

Love,

Robin

Dear Dad and Nora,

This morning regular activities were canceled and we all did one big project. The project was building a barrier between the mess hall and the infirmary, all the way down to the lake. It's tall—taller than I am. When we asked why we had to build it, the counselors were like, "You'll see!" and "Keep working!" The whole thing's very mysterious.

Maybe it has something to do with color war games, which happen the last week of camp. I don't know. Chloe says there wasn't anything like this last year. (She says the food was better last year too, and the bugs weren't nearly as bad.)

The barrier went up surprisingly fast, considering we're missing so many people. The infirmary's basically stuffed. At least no one who's stuck there is lonely. It must stink to be sick at camp.

I'm on my bunk now for quiet time—eating spray cheese, since I skipped lunch. Chloe's getting tired of spray cheese (weirdo), but she loves the cookies you made. Apparently after quiet time we'll be fortifying the barrier and starting another one. It's actually kind of fun, even if no one has any idea why we're doing it. Alanya says we can swim after, so we'll still get to do our silliest dive contest. YAY.

Love,

Robin

Dear Dad and Nora,

I'm pretty tired from all the barriers we've been building the past few days. When I finish this letter, I might take a nap. I especially could use one after last night, when I woke up to all these weird noises. It sounded like someone was out in the woods, moaning and banging on the barriers. Maybe it was raccoons, or one of the older kids playing a prank. Or scary stories from campfire getting to my head.

Whatever. It's gone now. Everything is less spooky in daylight.

Chloe got bitten by one of the bad mosquitoes, and the welt on her neck just keeps growing. She says it's itchier than any bite she's ever had, and she still hears the mosquito buzzing. I told her there aren't any evil bugs near her head, and she should eat spray cheese to keep them off in the future. She wrinkled her nose and said spray cheese sounds gross now.

She also said today's lunch meat smelled and tasted <u>good</u>, so maybe the bug bite poisoned her brain, haha. (Lunch smelled like onion farts and looked like moldy worms. I didn't eat it, but I can guess how it tasted.)

I gave her the calamine lotion you sent, and she slathered it on the welt. Hopefully that will do the trick.

Love,

Robin

Dear Dad and Nora,

Last night Chloe was acting really weird. Her eyes looked unfocused, and when she talked, I could barely understand a word she said. I told her she seemed really out of it, and she was like, "Sorry, I'm kind of a zombie today" (which sounded like, "Shrrray em kernder ugh zhahmeeter ay"), but she insisted she wasn't feeling worse, just worn down by the constant buzzing.

This morning her bunk was empty, and Alanya said she went to the infirmary. I can't believe I slept through that. I'm already lonely without her.

I asked if I could see her, but Alanya said no visitors allowed. Campers who aren't sick can't go past any of the barriers. It's almost like we built them to trap ourselves in.

Alanya says Chloe will be better soon, but no one who got sick has come back yet.

There are more campers gone than there are left. Plus whoever started that stupid prank is up half the night, moaning and howling. It's so annoying. Why can't they let us sleep?

I miss home. I miss biking to the quarry with Seth, playing fetch and tug with Peanut, and eating normal meals like the ones we have at home. That's how homesick I am—I would even give up spray cheese for a healthy, balanced diet! I wish I could sleep in my own bed.

Love,

Robin

Dear Dad and Nora,

Your letter and package did help me feel better, thanks. I especially loved getting Peanut's paw print. I've tacked it to the wall near my bunk. And I'm sure the earplugs will help.

Yes, I understand why you can't come get me early. And yes, I do have other friends here. But Chloe's still stuck in the infirmary, and it's not as much fun without her.

Morning activities are All Barriers All the Time now. I'm getting really strong from lifting so many sandbags, boards, and bricks, which is cool, but if I'd known Camp Dunmore would be like this, I might have gone to Girl Scout camp instead.

No one has gone to the infirmary in the past two days, but no one has come back from it, either. They've been spraying poison at night, so the mosquitoes are basically gone, but the counselors are still monitoring us all super carefully. They smear tons of cream on even small, regular bites. We're basically not allowed to get itchy.

I miss Chloe. I actually thought about sneaking out last night to see her, but when I peeked out the door, all the banging and wailing got louder, and I kind of freaked out.

Don't worry, I won't try that again.

Love,

Robin

Dear Dad and Nora,

I'm shaking while I write this, so hard I keep dropping the pen.

This morning part of the barrier was damaged. They sent me up a ladder to repair the top, which meant I could see partway over. I swear—swear—I saw Chloe in the woods. She was walking really strangely, like her legs were too stiff to bend. I called her name and she didn't look up, but I heard a groan.

I tried to climb over the barrier to get to her, but a counselor pulled me back to the ground. They said I must be dehydrated. That I'm overexcited and imagining things. They said Chloe went home last night.

So why are her things still here?

The counselor ignored my questions and sent me to the cabin to rest.

I did take a nap, but I woke up because of a loud crash outside. There were shouts and screams, then the screaming stopped, and now there's only moaning. So much moaning. And what sounds like something being dragged through the dirt.

Maybe it's just sandbags. But we're supposed to lift with our knees and carry those.

It's getting dark, which means I slept past dinner. Why didn't anyone come get me? I ate the last of the spray cheese and one of my two remaining brownies. I'm scared to go out there.

Please send more food, but also please come get me now. Please? I don't like it here anymore.

Love,

Robin

Dear Dad and Nora,

When I woke up this morning, the cabin was empty. No one came back last night. Not even Alanya.

The moaning has stopped and the sun is up, but I'm still afraid to go outside. I don't hear anyone out there, or see anyone out the windows—though it's hard to see much because the cabin has trees on all sides.

I ate the last brownie for breakfast, but I found another can of spray cheese that had rolled under Chloe's and my bunk bed. It feels about half empty. Or half full, as Nora would say. Haha.

I'm taking it as a sign. A sign I am meant to survive this.

There are five more days until camp ends. Five days before you're supposed to get me.

I can't wait here that long.

I'm going to walk west, away from the

lake. I'll take spray cheese, bug spray, a flashlight, and this letter. I'm taking Peanut's paw print too.

If this letter reaches you and I don't, please tell Peanut I love her.

I love you guys too. Not just because you send me spray cheese. :)

I'm going out there.

Wish me luck.

Love,

Robin

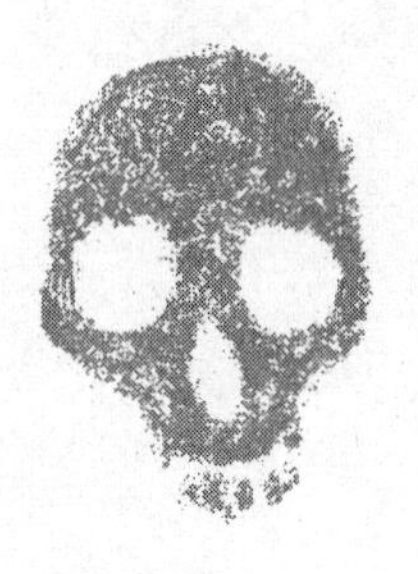

NO FEAR

There once was a boy
who wasn't afraid
of things that go bump in the night.

Even the spookiest wail
couldn't move him to
tremble or shiver with fright.

When cool winds blew
their breath on his neck,
the boy didn't worry or shudder.

He merely walked faster,
right past the grave
where they'd buried his four older brothers.

He seemed not to hear
the chorus of moans
that swirled in the air all around him.

He chose not to flinch
if he noticed the bones
—once fingers—that beckoned toward him.

This boy believed
in the core of his heart
he'd be safe from all things he ignored—

as if choosing to think not of rain
kept one dry
whenever it thundered and poured.
If others attempted to

raise the alarm,
the boy rejected them curtly,

reciting the words
he wanted to hear:
"What I do not believe in can't hurt me."

But having no fear was
foolish at best,
and he soon would be joining his kin.

For he might not believe
in ghosts or in ghouls—
but the monsters believed in him.

THE SECRET

Ava and Giuliana were the kind of friends who shared everything—including, and especially, their secrets.

Ava told Giuliana that she was the one who broke her mother's hair clip, and how relieved she was when it got blamed on her baby brother (who was still too young to get in trouble). Giuliana told Ava where she'd hidden her private journal, and sometimes even let Ava read it (though Ava already knew about most of the things inside). They told each other what they really thought of the books they read and the people they met and the things they heard on the news. They shared their dreams for the future. They shared their fears and worries too.

There was nothing Ava couldn't or didn't tell her best friend. But there was one thing Giuliana refused to tell Ava. It was the only secret they didn't share.

"What is it?" Ava asked. She leaned closer to Giuliana, though they were already side by side.

Giuliana shook her head. "I can't tell you."

Ava frowned and picked at a scab on her knee. "But you know all my secrets. I tell you everything about me!"

"I tell you everything about me too," Giuliana said. "You're my best friend. But I can't tell you this secret. I just can't."

"Please?" Ava begged. "I won't tell anyone, I swear."

"I know you wouldn't. But I *can't*. The secret won't let me."

Ava crossed her arms. "What do you mean it won't let you?"

Giuliana looked serious, and almost scared. She whispered, "I mean, the secret wants to stay secret. And if I tell you, for the secret to survive, we can't both survive too."

Ava shivered. "Are you saying the secret would *kill* me?" It was the strangest thing Giuliana had ever said. Ava wasn't even sure how that was possible. Maybe it was some kind of elaborate prank, or a game Giuliana was playing.

Giuliana blinked. "I didn't say that. But who knows? It's a powerful secret. Why take the risk? It's too dangerous."

Ava stood up. This was getting weird. She didn't really believe what Giuliana was saying, but she wanted to stop talking about it. Her friend clearly wasn't going to tell her the secret now anyway. She would have to ask another day.

"C'mon," Ava said. "Let's go play in the woods."

So they did.

Ava couldn't stop thinking and wondering about Giuliana's secret. The next week, she brought it up again. But again, Giuliana refused to spill.

"It's not that kind of secret," she said. "It can't be shared. We can't both know it."

Ava almost screamed with frustration. "Well, if the secret can't be told, where did you even hear it?" she asked.

Giuliana glanced over her shoulder as if to check no one else was listening. "I didn't hear it. No one told me," she said. "One day, I just knew it. Like the secret decided to live inside me." She lowered her voice even further. "Once I knew the secret, I had no choice but to keep it. That's how this secret works."

Ava felt a chill crawl up the back of her neck. Maybe she was glad not to know the secret. Maybe Giuliana was being a good friend by not sharing it. Just hearing about it was giving Ava the creeps.

Forty years passed in which they did not speak of it again.

They talked about everything else, though. Ava told Giuliana about her wife and three kids, and the things she liked most and least about her job, and the squirrel family that lived in her attic. Giuliana told Ava about her adventures traveling the world, and the last conversation she'd ever have with her dad, and the things her favorite music made her think about and feel. They shared all their hopes, dreams, fears, and regrets, and they still shared all their secrets. All except one.

Ava visited Giuliana and brought it up again. "Hey, remember that secret from when we were kids? The one you would never tell me?"

Giuliana looked surprised. "Of course I remember," she said. She poured more tea, and nudged the sugar in Ava's direction.

"Did you ever tell anyone what it was?" Ava asked.

Giuliana raised her eyebrows over the rim of her teacup. "Of course not," she said. "I wouldn't do that."

Ava smiled at her old friend. "Won't you please tell me now? I'm dying to know!"

Giuliana set down her cup. It rattled in its saucer. "Don't die to know! It's not worth it! That's what I keep telling you," she said sternly.

Ava giggled. But her friend looked deadly serious.

Ava rolled her eyes. "Come on, we're not kids anymore. You can't seriously believe the secret could kill one of us."

Giuliana shrugged and looked away. "It's a very powerful secret," she said. "I can't say what it will do. And besides, curiosity killed the cat."

The orange tabby on the ottoman purred.

"Maybe if you tell me, the secret's power will be weakened," Ava said.

Giuliana looked uncomfortable. "I don't think the secret would like that," she said.

Ava sipped her tea, hoping it would calm the unease in her stomach. "Where does the secret get its power from?" she asked.

But Giuliana would say nothing more about it.

Neither friend brought it up the whole rest of the week. But when Ava was leaving, Giuliana hugged her and said, "It's a terrible secret. You'd hate to know it. You should be glad I'm not telling you. You'd regret it. It's truly awful."

Ava resolved to never ask again.

Forty more years passed. Ava summoned Giuliana to her bedside.

"Old friend," Ava said, "I've had a long and

good life. We've had a long and good friendship. Now you're visiting me here on my deathbed. Will you please finally tell me the secret?"

Giuliana shook her head. "That would be the end of it," she said. "I don't dare."

Ava laughed. "Giuliana, I'm dying anyway. You can tell me now. There is nothing to be lost."

Giuliana stared at her best friend for a very long time. Ava stared back.

Giuliana let out a heavy sigh. "Very well," she said. "But don't say I didn't warn you. It's terrible."

They sent everyone else from the room.

Giuliana leaned close and whispered in Ava's ear. "Here's the secret," she said slowly. "The secret is, now that I've told you this, the secret is no longer a secret."

Ava held still. She waited for more. But Giuliana had finished talking.

"Wait," Ava said. "That's it? *That's* the secret you've been keeping all these years? The one you refused to share for our entire friendship?" Her heart pounded with anger. "You were right, that *is* awful. I wish you hadn't told me. You know, it's not even a clever joke. Or would you call that a riddle?"

Giuliana didn't answer.

Ava shook her head, still not believing what she'd heard. "Ha. Right. We can't both know it and live because then it's not a real secret anymore. Very funny." She turned to Giuliana. "Did you seriously think I wouldn't be mad when I heard that? Giuliana?"

But her best friend still didn't answer. She couldn't.

She'd told Ava the secret, and now Giuliana was dead.

LUCKY

Wade didn't think it was weird to eat worms. He didn't love the idea of squishing one in his teeth, or feeling it slither down his throat to squirm around in his belly—but if you thought about it that way, eating fish or cows or birds or pigs was weird too. Maybe even weirder.

But that's not why he ate the worm.

Back in preschool, Wade's class had sung a song about an old lady who swallows a fly, which somehow kills her—Wade wasn't clear on exactly how. He'd accidentally swallowed a tiny bug or two that flew into his mouth while he was playing outside, and he was fine. If his sister was to be believed, the average human swallows several spiders over the course of a lifetime, because spiders crawl into our mouths while we're sleeping. (Wade's mother said that wasn't true, but sometimes parents fudge the truth to shield their kids from it, he'd learned.)

Anyway, lots of people ate bugs on purpose. Wade's best friend, Sienna, had an aunt who ran a health-food store, and grasshopper flour was one of their bestselling products. According to Sienna, grasshoppers and crickets were nutritious and full of protein, and eating them was good for the planet too. Wade believed her.

But that's not why he swallowed the worm.

The kids who saw it happen figured Wade ate the worm to shut up the bully who'd dared him. It was true that while Marissa was dangling the worm in Wade's face, cooing "Open wide!" Wade wished she would stop and go away. And eating the worm seemed like the quickest way to achieve that.

But it wasn't Wade's idea—or Marissa's—for him to swallow the worm, really.

It was the worm's.

The worm didn't *say* it wanted Wade to gulp it, but as it writhed in Marissa's fingers, Wade felt what it needed so clearly, it was almost as though it had spoken. As soon as the thought of it entered Wade's head, he realized he wished for that too.

So he opened his mouth and the worm dropped in.

Marissa shrieked and ran away. Wade swallowed.

The worm slid down Wade's throat like pudding. It tasted earthy and wormy and noodly and right. He was instantly glad.

Wade imagined the worm curled up in his belly, warm and content, making itself at home. His bad day was suddenly better. He was keeping the worm safe.

It belonged with him.

Wade couldn't explain it. He didn't try. Not even to Sienna, and Wade told Sienna everything. At least, he had before the worm.

After Wade swallowed the worm, the teasing got worse. Anyone who hadn't seen it quickly heard about what happened. Wherever he went, kids shouted his new nicknames: Worm Eater. Worm Boy. Worm Breath. Squirmy Wormy.

Sienna walked around with her hands curled in fists, ready to defend him. But Wade shrugged. He didn't mind.

He didn't care anymore about nicknames. He only cared about dirt.

"You are what you eat," he told Sienna, and dropped down on her lawn and wiggled toward some mud. Sienna looked a little horrified, so Wade stood back up and brushed himself off. "Just kidding," he said. "I wouldn't let worms take over my brain. Ha! Haha!"

She gave him more distance after that.

It didn't matter. What mattered was keeping the worm happy.

He kept a baggy of soil and grass in his pocket, for times when it wanted a snack. He drank water only in small sips, well spaced out, so it wouldn't ever worry about puddles.

Alone in his bedroom, he practiced moving across the carpet, tightening and extending his muscles until his wiggles were more of a glide.

It felt good.

He felt chosen.

Like he and the worm were one.

"Freak," Marissa said whenever she saw him. Wade just smiled. She didn't know what she was missing. She didn't realize how empty she was.

Wade, though—Wade wasn't empty. Wade was fulfilled.

His worm had given him purpose.

He lay down on the ground near the fence at the edge of the playground. The cool, damp earth felt nice beneath his limbs. He dug in a little farther.

He turned his head to one side and burped. Several worms, tiny things, slid out of his mouth and into the dirt. Wade watched his worm babies fondly. They wriggled and searched for new places to grow.

He hoped, when it was time, they would find good companions.

Companions to host them. Companions to feed them. Companions to offer them love.

Those companions didn't know it yet, but each of them was lucky. Very lucky.

"Wade!" Sienna called from their usual spot by the swings. Wade ignored her. He had other things to do.

Wade burrowed his shoulders into the dirt. Mud filled his ears, but he still heard the sounds of his classmates at recess. "The worms crawl in, the worms crawl out!" their voices chorused.

Yes, he thought gladly. *Yes.*

The Best Teacher at Pleasant Hill Oak Elementary

Before Sydney and her dad moved in with Syd's grandma, Gram registered Syd to enter fifth grade at Pleasant Hill Oak Elementary School.

The move happened in late August—and happened quickly, it seemed to Syd. Time had stretched and lolled like it always did in summer. Then suddenly it jumped and was gone. There were only goodbyes, and lots of boxes, and pulling up the driveway to Gram's house, which was Sydney's house now too.

Gram was waiting for them, of course. So was Syd's favorite dinner, and a WELCOME HOME sign on the door. And a letter from the school saying Sydney was assigned to Ms. Eternity's class, and school would begin next week.

"Ms. Eternity!" Syd's dad said, reading over Syd's shoulder. "I had her for fifth grade too."

"As did I," said Gram.

Syd looked up. "No way. Shouldn't your teachers be retired by now?"

Gram laughed. "Oh, I don't think Ms. Eternity will ever retire. Teaching gives her life!" she said.

Syd slid down in her seat. An ancient teacher who'd been around forever didn't sound promising. Syd wished she hadn't had to change schools.

Dad squeezed her shoulder. "You'll see. Ms. Eternity's the best thing about Pleasant

Hill Oak Elementary."

"You're lucky to be in her class. She teaches history like she was there," Gram said.

"Probably because she *was*," Syd grumbled.

"Perhaps!" Gram shrugged cheerfully. "Anyone care for dessert?"

Syd folded up the letter and focused on pie.

On the first day of school, there were several surprises. First, she was one of two Sydneys in her class. She'd never met a kid with her same name before. The other Sydney was a boy, but that wasn't going to make things less confusing. He had the desk right behind hers, which meant when the teacher called on one Syd, she looked in both Syds' direction. It was funny the first time, but quickly became annoying.

Second, Ms. Eternity's classroom wasn't on the same floor as the others. It was down on "Level B," the school called it, as if that would stop everyone from noticing the classroom was in the basement. As in, belowground. As in, no windows and no sunlight and no staring outside when distracted. Ms. Eternity called it a "cave of learning." She said it like that was a good thing.

The third and biggest surprise was Ms. Eternity herself. She wasn't at all ancient like Sydney had expected. In fact, she seemed young. Well, young for a teacher. Certainly young for a teacher who'd been teaching since Gram was a kid. That part had to be a misunderstanding.

"Ms. Eternity seems great," Syd admitted when Gram and Dad asked how the first day had gone. "But she's definitely not the same teacher you both had in school. Maybe this Ms. Eternity is that Ms. Eternity's daughter or something." She crunched on a cream cheese and celery stick Dad had prepared for her snack.

Gram shook her head, and took a celery

stick too. "Ms. Eternity doesn't have children. She just looks young. She really drinks up the energy of her students, so to speak."

Ms. Eternity *had* been energetic, but Gram's explanation didn't cover it. "It can't be the same person," Syd insisted. She tugged the high neck of her shirt. She didn't mind school uniforms, but it was odd how the fifth graders all had to wear turtlenecks.

"Does your Ms. Eternity have dark, straight hair pulled back in a bun?" Dad asked.

"Yes," Sydney said. "But that doesn't prove anything."

"And very pale skin? And red-brown eyes? And long, pointed teeth?" Dad pressed.

Syd narrowed her eyes. Now that he mentioned it, the teacher's teeth *were* rather pointy. She'd seen them at lunchtime, when Ms. Eternity smiled before sipping from her thermos.

But still. "I'm telling you," Syd said, "it's impossible."

Gram and Dad exchanged a knowing look. "Impossible, eh?" Gram said. "Well, I have a feeling you'll be learning a lot this school year."

Gram was right. Sydney *was* learning a lot in fifth grade. By the end of each day, she felt drained of energy but full of knowledge. Ms. Eternity had a way of bringing every subject to life—not just history, like Gram had mentioned, but math, science, writing, and geography too. She was the best teacher Syd ever had, even though she was also the strangest.

When Sydney was in pre-K, she kind of thought all teachers lived at school. It wasn't an active thought, just a thing she'd assumed in the back of her mind, without really thinking it through. She only became aware she'd thought it when she ran into her pre-K teacher, Mr. ibnAle, at the grocery store. Syd was so surprised to see Mr. ibnAle outside the classroom, she'd yelped.

Before that moment, she hadn't realized teachers were normal people with normal lives, who lived in normal houses and shopped using normal shopping carts. She'd thought they were just . . . teachers. It had seemed almost wrong to see Mr. ibnAle in the produce aisle, holding three cucumbers like a *person* would.

It was funny to her now, the idea of teachers living at school. She pictured them filing into the supply closet at night and powering down until the custodian let them out in the morning. To her little-kid brain, that had made more sense than the alternative.

She knew better now, of course. But the longer Sydney spent in Ms. Eternity's classroom, the harder it was to picture the teacher outside it. Ms. Eternity never left the cave of learning during the school day. She didn't even join the class outside for recess. It was tough to imagine her in any aisle of the grocery store—she would look completely out of place. Besides, the only food Sydney had seen the teacher eat was whatever she drank from that thermos. She seemed to be on a special diet. More than anyone Syd had ever met, Ms. Eternity didn't belong in the normal-person world.

"Where does Ms. Eternity live?" she asked the other Syd one day when they were paired for a group project.

Other Syd shrugged. "I dunno," he said. "I've never seen her around town."

"Do you think she has pets?" Sydney asked. She pictured the teacher with a dog, a parakeet, a rabbit. None of those seemed right.

"Probably not," Other Syd said. "There's never any pet hair on her cape."

"What do you think she keeps in that big cabinet behind her desk?" Syd asked. She motioned at it with her chin. The sign above the lock said PRIVATE: KEEP OUT.

"Supplies?" Other Syd guessed. He scratched his head. Sydney hoped he didn't have lice. "I dunno. Could be something weirder," he said. "Ms. Eternity's pretty unusual."

"She is," Syd whispered. "I've noticed that too." But Other Syd said no more about it.

For Teacher Appreciation Week, Syd wanted to give Ms. Eternity something special. She spent a long time making her a card, depicting some of the things the teacher seemed most passionate about: Books. Bats. Fractions. The moon.

Syd picked up her red marker and thought about adding blood—they'd just done a science unit on the circulatory system, and how blood transports oxygen and nutrients through the body—but she worried it might look too gory. She put the marker down, and used a pen to write "Best Teacher Ever" inside.

Usually for Teacher Appreciation Week, Dad baked cookies or bought a gift certificate, but this time he handed Syd a jar of dark, thick liquid.

"What's this?" Sydney asked. "A smoothie?"

"It's Ms. Eternity's present," Dad answered. "Hold on, I'll get a bow."

"Gross! It looks like blood." Syd held the jar at arm's length.

Dad lifted both eyebrows. "Does it? Well, just give it to her. I have a feeling she'll like it."

Syd wrinkled her nose. Dad fastened a bow to the top.

"Don't yuck someone else's yum," Gram said. She handed Sydney her lunch bag.

Syd felt embarrassed bringing the jar to school, but Ms. Eternity seemed to like it almost as much as she liked the card. She unscrewed the lid, poured the liquid into her thermos, and took a giant swig. "Delicious! Please tell your father I said thank you," she said. She smiled and her teeth glistened.

In spring, when the weather warmed up, Sydney joined the track team. Gram had suggested it as a way of keeping her energy up—by the end of each school day, Syd always felt sapped and sluggish. "Fifth grade is like that," Gram said. "Running will help." And it did.

The last week of school, the students cleaned out their desks and helped Ms. Eternity pack up the classroom. Syd raised her hand. "What are you doing over the summer?" she asked.

"Oh," Ms. Eternity said. "Getting lots of rest."

"Will you go anywhere?" Other Syd asked.

"Nope! I'll be right here," the teacher said. "Without you kids around to keep me full of life, summers are pretty low-key." She picked up a stack of papers. "Let's talk about summer reading."

On the last day of school, Ms. Eternity gave each student a book they could take home to keep. Sydney's book had three friends on the cover. Other Sydney's book had a girl captaining a pirate ship.

Other Syd peeked over Syd's shoulder. "Maybe when we've finished, we can trade and read both," he said.

Syd smiled. "Great idea."

After school, Syd ran the last track meet and hugged Gram and Dad at the finish line. "All done with fifth grade," Dad said. His eyes looked misty. "Ready to go home, champ?"

"Yup," Sydney said. "Wait, no! I forgot my book. Hold on, I've got to go get it." She ran into the building and down to Level B. Ms. Eternity's classroom was empty, but luckily the door was unlocked. Syd stepped inside.

Huh, she thought. *So Ms. Eternity* does *leave the classroom.* She smiled to herself. How silly she'd been to imagine otherwise.

It was sad and strange, seeing the room where she'd had her best year yet all packed up and put away, so it could be cleaned and made fresh for next year's fifth grade. Syd felt jealous of those new students. She almost wished she could stay in Ms. Eternity's class forever.

Syd looked in her desk, hoping to find the book, but the desk was empty too. She looked on all the shelves, and in the other desks, but the book was nowhere to be found. She eyed the big cabinet behind the teacher's desk. Maybe it had gotten put away there?

Syd walked toward the cabinet. The PRIVATE: KEEP OUT sign was still in place, but the key was right there in the lock. Syd could turn it and just take a peek. She was only looking for her book—she wouldn't go through anything else. She wasn't snooping.

Syd reached for the key. She turned it, and heard a click. The heavy door swung open.

Syd gasped. She shoved the door shut as quickly as she could, and scrambled to lock it. She forgot about her book, and bolted from the room. She ran up the steps and out of the building, faster than she'd run in any race. Her heart pounded hard and her lungs gasped for breath. She didn't slow down until she'd reached her dad's minivan.

Dad and Gram peered out the window. "Find your book?" Gram asked.

Syd shook her head and bent over to catch her breath. "You look tired," Dad said. "It's been a big year. Let's get you home and filled up with a snack."

Syd straightened. Gram winked. "I hope you didn't disturb Ms. Eternity. Teachers work hard! They deserve a peaceful summer."

"Right," Syd said. She blinked in the bright sunlight, and climbed into the minivan. She *was* tired. She did need a snack. She was probably a little delirious from the track meet and the last day's excitement. It was making her mind play tricks on her.

When she'd opened the teacher's cabinet,

she could have sworn she saw something impossible: Ms. Eternity, tucked inside, with her arms across her chest, her eyes closed, and her body and face still. Except . . . she'd lifted one finger to her lips to say *shhhhhh*.

Or had she?

Sydney pushed the image from her brain. That couldn't have happened. Teachers didn't live at school. They certainly didn't sleep inside cabinets lined with silk. *Feeding off her students' energy* was just an expression.

Syd smiled at her own imagination.

She breathed in and felt the oxygen move through her bloodstream, just like Ms. Eternity had taught them.

ONCE UPON A TIME

Once upon a time, it was a dark and stormy night.

Trees rattled their branches like skeletons shake their bones.

Raindrops pounded the windows like they wanted to get inside.

The wind howled and moaned, as if some-one had stepped on its toe.

Sophia ignored all this. She wasn't listen-ing to the storm outside. She was too busy reading her book.

The story in the book involved a room in a house a lot like Sophia's. There was an armchair in a living room with a bookcase and a reading lamp, just like the room she was in. There was a large black cat curled up near the story's fireplace—much like Whiskers, the cat on the rug at Sophia's feet, who sometimes opened his eyes to slits and checked if she was still reading. There was a storm outside with lightning and thunder. But there wasn't a girl in the story yet. There didn't seem to be any humans in the book at all.

Sophia turned the page. The fire crackled beside her, and its shadows danced through the room. She wiggled her toes in her thick socks. She was interested in the story, but she wasn't sure where it was going. Nothing much seemed to be happening yet. She hoped it would pick up soon.

Sophia's father always said of his daughter, "That girl loves getting lost in a book. Sometimes she's so wrapped up in the stories she's reading, we almost can't pull her out of them."

He was exaggerating, of course, but she did love that feeling—when a book felt so real to her, she was practically living inside it. When the world of a story seemed more present and true than the world she was actually part of.

The best books often caused that feeling in Sophia. But this book wasn't one of them, not so far. Its story seemed to have something missing.

Sophia started the next chapter. A door in the story creaked open, but before anyone stepped through it, a crash of thunder exploded in the room where Sophia was reading. It startled her so completely, she dropped the book on the floor. Whiskers' eyes flew open and his fur stood on end. He ran from the room, leaving Sophia alone by the fire.

Sophia leaned over and picked up the book. She flipped through the pages, looking for the spot where she'd left off. Sophia had read a lot of books, so she knew—when a door in the story creaked open, something strange was about to happen. She wanted to find out what.

The next sentence was interrupted by an eerie, spooky sound—like a thousand ancient pages rustling and the secrets inside them crying out. It sounded far off, but it *felt* like it was right behind her.

Sophia looked up from the book. "What was that?" she whispered.

"It's nothing," the sound whispered back.

Sophia jumped to her feet. The hairs on her neck leaped up too.

She peeked behind the armchair.

No one was there.

"It's not nothing!" she said to the empty room, feeling a chill despite the fire. She desperately wished her cat were still beside her.

"It's nothing," the sound repeated. Its voice

was half whimper, half shriek. It reminded Sophia of nails on a chalkboard

and loneliness

and the wind.

Sophia's heart thudded loudly, but she would not show her fear. She put her hands on her hips. "I know what I heard," she said.

"Do you?" asked the sound. It seemed to be coming from all around her. It was outside, yet *inside*, her head.

"It's nothing," the sound said. "Nothing's happening. Nothing's happening." As it spoke, the pages of the book she'd been reading rippled.

Sophia slammed it shut. She stomped her foot. "Enough!" she said, sounding tougher than she felt.

The book fell back open. The *nothing* became a laugh.

"The story needs you," the sound whispered. "It needs more character. Come inside.

Without you, nothing can happen. A book without a reader might as well not exist."

Sophia wanted to scream. She wanted to hide. But she was frozen—unable to look away from the book. Its pages reached for her and pulled her in deeper, closer.

Something's happening, she thought.

"Something's happening," the story whispered. It wrapped itself around her until she was lost in it completely.

The next morning, the storm had passed. Sunlight streamed into the empty room and warmed the cold ashes in the fireplace.

Sophia's father entered and picked up the book lying open on his favorite armchair. He couldn't remember having left it there—perhaps it had been the cat. Whiskers was acting so strangely today. He may well have knocked it off the shelf.

Sophia's father glanced at an illustration

at the bottom of the open page. There was a wide-eyed girl in a nightgown and knee socks. He supposed the story must be about her. She reminded him of someone he knew. But who was it?

He shook his head. He couldn't remember. Maybe it was someone he'd only read about. You never knew who you'd meet in a book.

Sophia's father looked around the room and wondered why he felt something was missing.

He closed the book, slid it onto the bookshelf, and turned out the reading light.

GOOD DOG AND BAD CAT: THE SCARIEST TAIL

Am very good dog. Humans all say so.

My kid says "Good dog" while scritching under chin and between ears how likes it. My kid gives nice scritches. My kid is BEST.

Top job as dog is: protect kid!

Sleep next to kid's bed. Patrol house and yard. Greet and approve visitors. Bark away mail. Chase off squirrels.

Watch! Notice! Smell! Listen!

Also: fetch balls, clean plates, and take

naps in sunbeam.

Today during sunbeam, CAT appears. Cat inside! Kid is happy. Cat gone for days. Now cat back! I greet hello. But WAIT. ALERT!

Cat is WRONG.

Cat looks like right cat. Cat moves like right cat. Cat sounds like right cat. But cat NOT smell like right cat.

I sniff closer. Cat smells strange. Cat smells rotten. Bad cat is NOT approved.

I tell kid.

Kid says "Sit" and "Stay" and "Down" and "No barking."

But CAT!

Kid not listen.

Cat weaves through kid's legs and gives dog LOOK. I whine.

Kid says "Shhh."

Kid pets cat. Gives cat scritches! I growl.

Cat hisses. I arf! Am put outside.

No fair.

I wait next to door and sit to remind: Am good dog! Protects!

Time pass.

Kid lets dog in. Cat purrs. Dog not fooled. Cat is trouble. Cat tail twitches.

Doorbell rings! Friend here. I greet. Friend approved!

Kid turns on noise box. Kid and friend play game. Cat watches. I watch cat.

Time pass.

Gets dinner! Cat too. Kid eats. I sit by kid.

Kid gives scraps! Says am good dog. Wags to thank. Gets scritches! Feels happy. Licks kid's face. Face delicious! Tastes like CHEESE. Feels happy. Remembers cat. Flattens ears.

Cat is watching.

Cat is planning.

Dog can smell it.

Cat no good.

Tells kid! Kid not listen.

Cat looks hungry. Cat just ate! Dog worries.

Stays close to kid.

Friend gets square. Square for game! Game for kids. Kid says "Ouija!"

Cat looks glad. Dog not like it.

Square goes on floor. Thing goes on top. Kid touches thing. Friend touches thing. Friend asks question.

Nothing happen.

Kid giggles. Friend giggles. Cat narrows eyes. Thing moves.

DOG HAIRS UP.

Kid surprised. Friend surprised.

Cat not surprised.

Cat stays focused.

Whiskers twitch. Thing moves again. Cat is . . . moving thing? But with brain?

How does do that??? And why?

Thing keeps moving. Kid says letters. Thing spells WORDS. Friend excited. Cat looks pleased.

Dog says ARF! Is told quiet.

Friend asks questions. Thing spells WORDS.

Kid untouch thing. Repeats thing words. Friend shivers. Cat waits.

Friend says, "Should we?"

Kid not sure.

Cat goes closer.

Cat rubs friend. Cat rubs kid. Lets out purr. Points with tail.

Friend stands up.

Kid gets flashlight.

Dog barks "NO!"

Kid not listen.

Cat tail swishes.

Out we go.

Moon is round. Night is quiet. Dog not like it.

Cat leads way.

Cat smells eager. Friend smells nervous. Kid excited. Also scared.

Cat walks in shadows. Moves back out.

Dog not trust this. Cat has PLAN. Plan smells suspicious. Cat smells BAD.

Sniffs air harder. Sees air move! White like cloud. Smells like danger!

Dog whines. Kid says "Shush." Cloud moves closer. Cloud smells BAD.

Kid grabs friend. Does see it too? Moves like cat tail. Moves like snake. Cat walks faster. Goes toward cloud!

Friend follows. Kid follows. Dog follows.

Does not like this.

Kid not see cloud. Cloud wraps kid ankle!

Must stop cloud! Must protect kid!

Says ARF!

Cloud retreats. Cat back arches. Cat shows fangs. ARFs again!

Cloud smell fades. Kid pulls leash. Dog not budge. Protects kid!

Cat looks mad.

Friend looks mad.

Kid looks mad.

Dog not care. Cat NOT win.

Kid turns around! Walks toward home! Dog comes too! Wig-wags tail! Leaves cloud behind! Does save the day! Is such good dog! Stops bad cat plan! Saves kid from danger!

Kid opens gate. Dog walks inside. Dog so happy! Cat so not.

Kid gives scritches. Says "Good dog." Dog wags thank you. Kid shuts gate.

NO.

WAIT.

Kid is outside. Dog is inside. Dog is stuck! KID WALKS AWAY.

Dog says ARF! Kid not listen. Kid says "Stay." Dog not believe this.

Kid goes with friend. Kid goes with cat. Kid goes toward cloud. Leaves dog behind!

Dog is trapped. Dog can't go. Bad cat has kid. Oh no oh no.

Arfs.

Whines.

Paces.

Sits.

Time pass.

Time pass.

Time pass.

Time pass.

Kid gone.

Friend gone.

Cat gone.

Dog here.

Waits for kid. Sniffs for kid. Whines for kid. Wishes KID.

Time pass.

No kid.

Time pass.

No kid.

Time pass.

WANTS KID!

Dog waits.

Dog waits.

Dog waits.

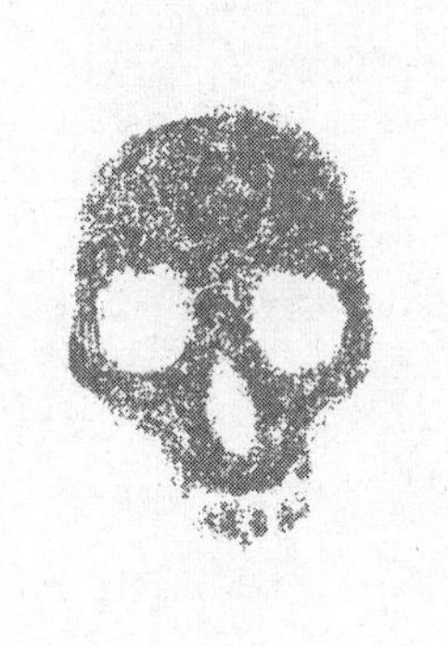

ONLY A DREAM

In her dream, there are no monsters.

Her mother puts away the axe and forgets about revenge.

Her father's smile reaches his eyes. There is no fear in them, no bitterness.

Her heart doesn't flood with regret.

Her baby brother is there, and he is himself, not some *thing*. He's not lost and replaced with a boy made of straw who drips pieces of himself where he toddles.

He blinks and laughs, and his eyes aren't

made of coal. No one asks her to sacrifice everything to save him. The impossible choice is unnecessary. He never disappeared in the first place.

In her dream, she did not climb those attic stairs. She doesn't find the box she's been told not to touch. It doesn't call to her. It doesn't whisper ancient verses only her ears can hear.

She doesn't blow off the dust. She doesn't want—no, *need*—to open it.

She won't turn the key or lift the top and release the family curse. Of course not.

It does not terrify and excite her.

It doesn't exist at all.

In the dream, she doesn't hide what she's done or confess it far too late. She will not utter the wish or blurt the promise that only make everything worse.

There is no need.

There are no monsters.

You couldn't say the real monster is she.

She is safe in her bed, and it's a beautiful new day. Songbirds sing to welcome it.

But then she wakes up.

The first thing she sees is darkness.

The second thing makes her close her eyes and scream.

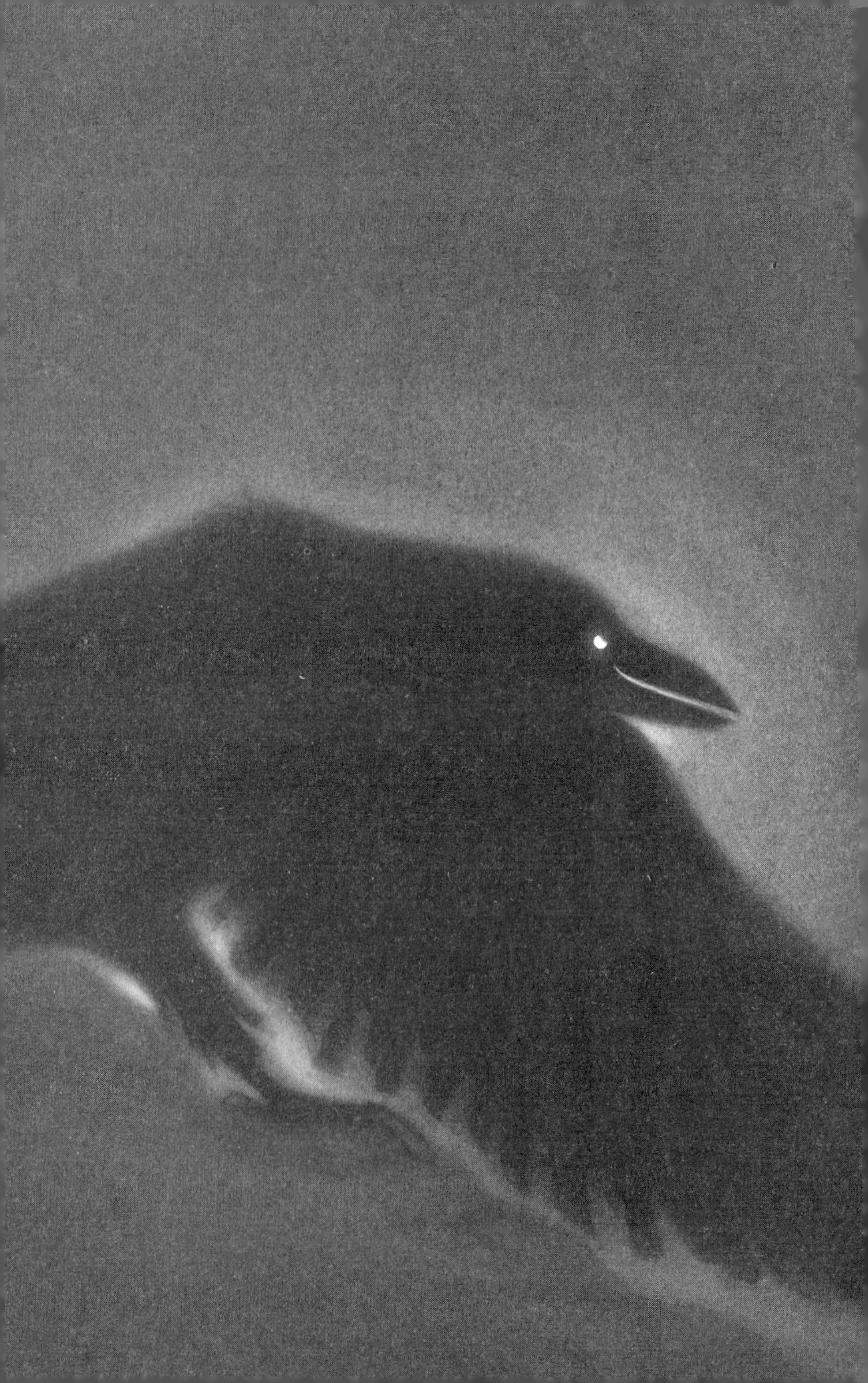

The Girl and the Crow

The girl wasn't sure why she didn't trust the crow. The girl's mother found him charming. The crow found himself charming too. But the girl found it best to avoid him.

For the most part, this wasn't hard. She ignored the crow and the crow ignored her. Until one day he didn't.

The girl was in the den, inventing a story about a witch, a fairy, and a troll. She was so wrapped up in her interesting thoughts, she didn't notice the bird until he spoke.

"What are you doing?" he asked.

She looked up and saw him perched on the mantelpiece. She resisted the urge to shoo him away.

"I'm making a story," she said. "About—" She tried to catch the thread of what she'd been thinking, but the idea had flown off when the crow interrupted. The girl could not fly after it.

The crow wasn't interested in her story anyway. "I'm bored," he said. "Entertain me."

"Um, okay," the girl said. "Would you like to play a game?"

"Oh, yes," the crow said. He tilted his head. "In fact, I'm already playing one."

The girl frowned. "What's the game?" she asked.

He danced in place. "That's for me to know and you to find out. You're a clever girl—more clever than you look. I'm sure you'll catch on eventually."

"Hey!" The girl crossed her arms. She didn't like insults and riddles.

The crow ruffled his feathers. "It's a compliment," he said. "Don't get in a huff. Usually, when one is complimented, one says thank you."

The girl hesitated. This felt like a trap. But her mother hadn't raised her to be rude. "Thank you?" she said.

The crow blinked. "You're welcome." He jumped from the mantelpiece to her shoulder. The girl froze.

The crow used his beak to rearrange the girl's hair. He tucked her curls behind her ear. She pretended it wasn't happening. She was still too stunned to move.

The crow grabbed a few hairs and, with a quick tug, yanked them out.

"Ow!" the girl cried. "That hurt!"

The crow shrugged and dropped the strands to the floor. "I need them. They'll be perfect in my nest."

"But they're mine," the girl said. "You can't just take them." She tried to nudge him off, but he ignored her.

He helped himself to more. The girl yelped.

"Don't be selfish," the crow said. "You've got plenty. Haven't you been taught it's nice to share?"

The girl's scalp tingled with shame.

She glanced around for a way to distract him. He might leave her alone if she found a better offering.

Her gaze fell on her own wrist. She took off the bracelet she'd been given for her birthday. "Look," she said. "Isn't this pretty? Why don't you take it for your nest instead?"

She dangled the loop of silver and gold. It glistened in the light. The bird considered it.

The girl held her breath.

"I don't want that," the crow said. "I'll take

this." He pecked the girl's cheek like it was an apple for him to devour.

Shocked tears stung her eyes, but the girl did not cry out. Maybe this would end if she acted like it didn't matter.

He pecked again.

"Stop," the girl whispered.

The crow cackled. He was having fun.

Of course he was. He'd invented this game.

He hopped to her other shoulder. "Your tears are so shiny. I love shiny things."

Before the girl could react, he pecked out her eyes. Her fingers flew to the empty sockets.

"No!" she screamed. "Stop! Enough!"

The crow laughed again. She reached out and grabbed him. He didn't struggle.

He didn't take her seriously enough to struggle.

"Caw! Caw!" he said. She couldn't see him, but she felt his glee.

The girl shuddered.

She wasn't playing.

She twisted her hands and heard a quick *snap*. The mocking stopped. The crow's body went limp.

"Enough," the girl whispered.

She dropped the dead bird. The game was over, but her heart filled with fear.

How could she explain this to her mother?

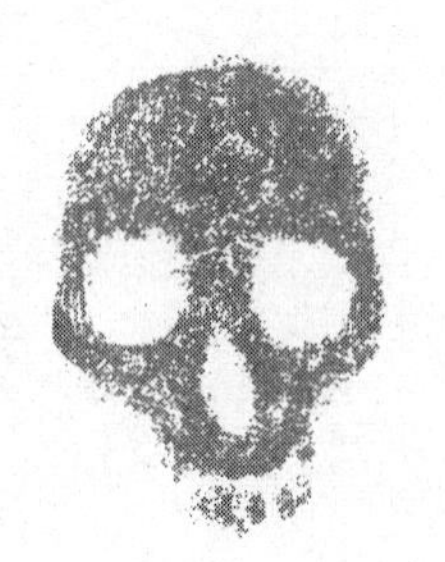

Renie's Song

Shhh . . . Did you hear that?
Yes, that! No, don't listen—

It's Renie's unfortunate song.
It sticks in your head,
round and round till you're dead,
and you'd better not get a note wrong.

Poor Renie's been cursed with no choice
but to hum

the same tune—back to back—dusk till
dawn.
If she pauses to take even one shaky breath,
darker trouble will soon come along.

The only way out
is to find a new ear
into which she can empty the curse:
a listener who,
after hearing the chorus,
might sing along with the verse.

If the song catches you,
your best hope—so I'm told—is:
Keep looping and looping it through.
Because if you come
to the end of the tune,
well—
it's the end of you too.

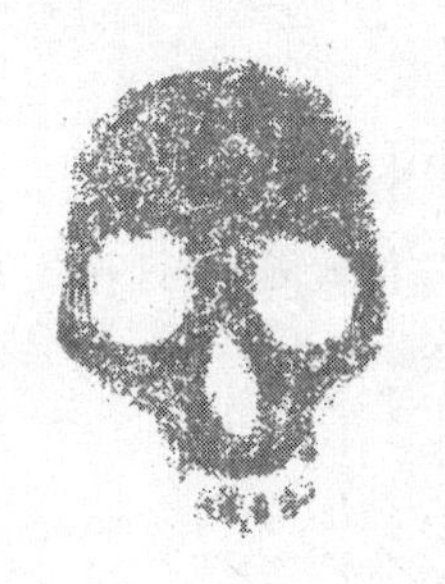

HERE, KITTY KITTY

When Erika and Mum moved into their new house, the first thing Erika unpacked was her trusty night-light. She plugged it into the socket by her bed and turned the switch. The bulb lit up with a warm, familiar glow. It made the new place feel like home already.

Erika didn't actually sleep with the night-light on anymore. She mostly used it for shadow puppets, truth or dare mood lighting, or as a post-bedtime reading light. But in all the places she and Mum had lived, the night-light was a constant. It felt comforting and good to plug it in here too, in this new old house where they would stay a lot longer. Erika and Mum weren't renting this time. Mum had purchased the house for a lucky price, and the plan was to live there forever.

Erika unpacked her clothes and put them away in the dresser. She unpacked Ribbit, the stuffed rabbit she'd had since she was a baby, and placed her on the bed. She unpacked her books and lined them up by color. Then she was bored with unpacking, so she went outside to explore.

Behind the old house, she found a field with tall grass and three gnarled apple trees. She ran to the first tree and jumped to grab the lowest branch. The tree looked perfect for climbing.

Erika swung her legs and climbed as high as she could. She picked a ripe apple and took a noisy bite. She was so focused on the tart, sweet fruit and the crunch of her own chewing, she didn't notice the stranger approaching the tree until the woman called out, "Hello there!"

Erika nearly fell off her perch. She regained her balance just in time.

"Sorry," the woman said. "I didn't mean to startle you. I'm Sam. I live over there." She pointed at the house next door.

"Hi." Erika squinted down at Sam, who looked about Erika's grandmother's age. She had short white hair and medium-brown skin that crinkled around her eyes when she smiled. "I'm Erika."

"I know," Sam said. "Your mom told me. It will be nice to have neighbors again after all these years. That house has been empty a long, long time."

"It has?" Erika hadn't thought about who owned the house before them.

"Oh, yes. More than fifty years. The last time anyone lived there, I was as young as you are now, if you can believe that," Sam said. "So was Robbie."

Erika jumped down from the tree, and brushed her hands off on her pants. "Who's Robbie?" she asked.

"Robbie's my friend who lived in your house. Roberta, her name was, but she hated that. She always went by Robbie. She grew up in your house, and I grew up in mine."

"And then she moved away?" Erika guessed.

A funny look crossed Sam's face. "No, not exactly," she said. "She got sick. All of a sudden. One day she was fine, and the next she could barely stand up. I brought her all the schoolwork she'd missed, but she never got a chance to complete it."

"She *died*?" Erika said. "In my house?"

Sam nodded slowly. "We were only twelve. Her parents boarded up the house and left in the middle of the night. They were so filled with grief, they never even said goodbye."

"I'm sorry," Erika said, because Sam still looked sad, even though all those years had passed.

"I used to think I still saw her waving to me from her window, though of course that was just wishful thinking, and maybe a trick of the light," the neighbor said.

"Oh." Erika didn't love the sound of that. It was one thing for someone to have died in the house. It was another thing entirely for that person to still be around. "Which window was hers?"

"That one." Sam pointed. "Second floor. Next to the small bathroom window."

Erika stared at the row of windows, and an uneasy feeling slid up her spine. Maybe because two of those windows were to *her* room.

"I think I hear my mom calling," she said. "Gotta go. Nice meeting you!" She ran to the house without waiting for Sam's reply. When she reached the back door, she glanced over her shoulder. The neighbor was gone.

Erika and Mum celebrated the first night in their house with waffles for dinner and a movie on the couch. When the movie was over, Erika brushed her teeth and went to bed, and fell into a deep sleep. She dreamed of apple trees and rocking chairs, and the *scratch scratch scratch* of someone—or something—scraping the wall next to her bed. The dream stopped when she woke up. The scratching sound did not.

She opened her eyes and saw it was still dark. Raindrops pounded on the windows. She blinked in the darkness and heard it again: *scratch scratch scratch*. It sounded like it was coming from a few feet away—like, right at the foot of her bed.

There are no monsters under the bed, she told herself. *Old houses have strange noises. There's definitely nothing there.* She clutched her stuffed rabbit closer. The scratches came again.

Erika held her breath. Slowly, slowly, and still hugging Ribbit, she peeked over the edge of the bed. Two yellow eyes stared back at her.

Erika yelped and turned on the night-light. Her eyes adjusted just in time to see a fluffy gray cat flick its tail and disappear.

She shook her head in disbelief. How had a *cat* gotten into her room? She almost didn't trust that she'd really seen it. Maybe her brain was still asleep and dreaming.

"Here, kitty kitty," she said softly. The cat did not return.

Erika looked at her open bedroom door. She considered getting up to go search for the creature, but she didn't quite want to explore her new old house at night. And if she did find the cat, what would she do? Put it outside in the rain? Wake up Mum and ask if they could keep it? No. If the cat was still around, it could wait until morning. At least the scratching noise had stopped.

She settled under her blankets, left the night-light on, and willed herself back to sleep.

In the morning, the rain was gone, and there was no sign of the night visitor. Thinking of it in daylight, the cat seemed much less spooky, though no less mysterious. Erika told her mother about it at breakfast.

"Maybe it snuck inside while the movers were bringing in boxes," Mum said. "Or maybe there was an open window or a loose board."

"Then where is it now?" Erika said.

Mum shrugged. "Cats can fit through all sorts of tiny spaces. They just kind of pour themselves in. It's pretty amazing. I think they might actually be liquid."

Erika giggled. She wondered if the kitty was as soft as it had looked.

That afternoon, she saw Sam outside weeding her garden. Sam waved and offered her some sugar snap peas. "Do you have a cat?" Erika asked.

"Nope, no pets," Sam said. "Just the crows and deer that visit the garden."

"Oh. I saw a gray cat yesterday. A small, fluffy one. Do you know whose it might be?" she said.

"Ah," Sam said. "That must be Ghost."

"A ghost?" Erika repeated.

Sam chuckled. "No, not a ghost. Ghost! That's the cat's name. She was Robbie's pet. Every once in a while, I see her around here. Mostly at night."

Erika narrowed her eyes. "But . . . that's impossible, right? That the cat was Robbie's? Cats don't live fifty years."

Sam shrugged. "They do have nine lives, some say. Maybe Ghost's lives all stretched back-to-back. Stranger things have happened."

Erika couldn't tell if the neighbor was kidding. "They have?" she said cautiously.

"Well, sure. Or maybe it's a different cat. But Ghost was always a strange one. Appearing and disappearing out of nowhere, without making a sound. Robbie's the only one she would let pet her, too. They were close, so close. When Robbie's parents moved, Ghost stayed behind. I think she didn't want to leave Robbie alone, so she hid."

"Didn't want to leave Robbie, even though Robbie was dead?" Erika said.

Sam nodded. "Animals know things we don't. They sense it."

Erika didn't ask what *it* was. She was pretty sure she didn't want to know.

She thanked Sam for the peas and walked back to the house, looking up at Robbie's window—her own window now. Or . . . was it? With a start, she realized something odd.

There were three regular windows and one

small one on the second floor. Erika's bedroom had two windows in it. The bathroom had one small one. So where did the extra window lead to? There were only two rooms on that side of the house—at least, only two Erika knew of.

She ran inside and up the stairs. She couldn't find any more rooms. But she didn't see a fourth window, either.

"Mum!" she called. "Mum, come quick!"

Her mother appeared, out of breath and looking worried. Erika felt bad that she'd scared her. "It's nothing terrible," she said. "Just weird." She explained about the extra window. Mum went outside with her to look, and back inside to double-check.

"You're right," Mum said. "How strange. That window must lead to another small room between your room and the bathroom. But there's no door. Maybe it got plastered over. I wonder why."

Mum knocked a few times on Erika's

bedroom wall, and pressed her ear against it. "It doesn't seem to be a load-bearing wall. I bet we can knock it down and make your room a few feet larger. We'll try tomorrow," she said. "Actually, this is a lucky find."

"Can I watch?" Erika asked.

Mum smiled. "Sure. You can even help."

That night, Erika dreamed of doorways upon doorways, opening opening opening but leading to nowhere. She woke to a familiar sound. *Scratch scratch scratch.* She opened her eyes. Moonlight streamed in through the windows.

She leaned over the side of the bed. "Here, kitty kitty." The fluffy gray cat stared back at her. "Is that you, Ghost?" she said.

The cat's ears twitched. Erika reached out a hand to pet her, but the kitty ducked away. She scratched at the wall with her paw, like it was a door she wanted Erika to open.

"Tomorrow," Erika told the cat. "We'll knock down the wall tomorrow."

The cat blinked at her. Her whiskers quivered. She vanished so quickly, Erika didn't even see her leave.

She told her mother about the sighting at breakfast. "Sounds like she's a stray with some claim to the place," Mum said. "You know, I've been thinking we might get a dog, now that we have our own house. There's no reason you couldn't have a cat too."

"Really?" Erika said.

Mum nodded. "Remind me and I'll pick up some cat food at The Galley. Maybe if we feed her, she'll decide she'd like to stick around."

Erika didn't mention the cat might already belong to a dead girl. She was sure the neighbor was mistaken or pulling her leg. But she might call the cat Ghost anyway. It was a good name for a cat with a talent for appearing and disappearing.

When the breakfast things were put away, Erika and Mum covered Erika's bed with a cloth and moved it away from the wall. Mum made a few tests and adjustments, made sure both their dust masks were in place, and handed Erika a sledgehammer. "Give it a good whack," she said. "Right there in the middle. Let's see if we can break through to the other side."

Erika lifted the sledgehammer. It was heavy, but the weight felt good in her hands. She stood in the spot where the kitty had been, and swung at the wall with all her might. The sledgehammer landed with a thunk.

"Again," Mum said. A few chunks of plaster crumbled to the floor.

She hit the wall a second time, and a third. On the fourth swing, the sledgehammer broke through. Mum cheered, then gasped as a spiderweb of cracks spread out from the hole and filled the entire wall. Erika had only a second to drop the sledgehammer and step back before the whole wall fell to the ground.

She stared. Where the wall once stood there was only a cloud of dust. Through the cloud, she could make out a small room with a small bed, and a rocking chair by the window. In the chair sat a skeleton of what once had been a person, who must have been about her size. The skeleton was looking right at them.

Erika gulped and moved closer to Mum. Behind them came a howl that made them both jump. The gray cat sprang out of nowhere and ran toward the chair. She meowed at the feet of the skeleton, and leaped into its lap. The kitty curled up on the skeleton's legs, settling against the bones. The chair rocked.

"Ghost," Erika whispered, and clutched her mother's arm. The cat closed her eyes. This was what she'd wanted.

The skeleton lifted a bony hand and stroked the cat's back.

Over the sound of her own heartbeat, Erika heard the kitty purr.

THE FRIEND

The best thing about summer was going to Nana and Vovó's house. And the best thing about Nana and Vovó's house was spending time with cousins. But when Anna Luiza's dad dropped her off at the start of August, most of her cousins weren't there yet—and Nana and Vovó had the flu.

"We're so glad you're here, though I'm sorry I can't hug you yet," Vovó said. She blew her nose and added the tissue to the mountain growing by her bedside.

"We'll be back on our feet in a day or two," Nana promised. She adjusted her many pillows. "Do you think you can help out with Silvana in the meantime?"

"Of course," Anna Luiza said. Silvana was the youngest of the eight cousins. As the oldest, Anna Luiza was used to being in charge.

"She's very responsible," her father confirmed. "Let me make you some tea with honey, then I'd best be on my way. Anna Luiza, you'll call if it turns out you need me?"

"Yup," Anna Luiza said. She left him with his parents and went downstairs to find her little cousin.

Silvana was in the music room, playing Candy Land on the floor. She hugged Anna Luiza's legs when she entered.

"Oh, gosh," Anna Luiza said. "You're playing Candy Land by yourself? You must be bored stiff with Nana and Vovó stuck in bed."

She plopped down next to her cousin.

Silvana advanced her game piece onto a yellow square. "I'm not playing by myself. I'm playing with Brucie."

Anna Luiza glanced around. "Who's Brucie?" It certainly looked like Silvana was playing alone.

"He's my friend," Silvana said.

"Ah." Anna Luiza vaguely remembered having an imaginary friend when she was Silvana's age. Her imaginary friend had been a unicorn with a rainbow mane, sparkly hooves, and a smart purple bow tie. Anna Luiza had called her Daffodil. "What does Brucie look like?" she asked.

Silvana made a face to say it was a silly question. "Like himself," she said. "Like a normal kid, but blurrier."

"Oh. Cool." Anna Luiza nodded seriously. When she was little, she always hated when adults acted like the things she said were cute or funny. She never did that to Silvana. "So do you want to play another game now that I'm here, or—"

"Yes!" Silvana cheered. "Brucie wants to play Go Fish."

Anna Luiza opened her grandmothers' game drawer and found a deck they could use. She shuffled the special way Nana had taught her, without bending any cards. "You and Brucie can be one team and I'll be the other."

Silvana frowned. "No teams. Three players is better than two."

Anna Luiza dealt three piles of five cards each, and let Silvana have her way. "Youngest goes first. Is that you or Brucie?"

"Me," Silvana said. She picked up her cards, arranged them carefully, and turned to the empty space between them. "Brucie, do you have any threes?"

After a pause, she took a card from the draw pile, and looked at Anna Luiza. "He doesn't. Your turn."

"Uh . . . do you want to check his cards to make sure?" Anna Luiza asked. Brucie's hand still lay where she'd dealt it.

Silvana shrugged. "Nope. I believe him."

"Okay." Anna Luiza looked at her own cards. "Do you have any jacks?"

"Me or Brucie?"

"You," Anna Luiza said. Silvana handed her one. "Thanks. Um, Brucie, do you have any jacks?"

Silvana selected a facedown card from Brucie's pile and handed it to her cousin. Anna Luiza took it. To her surprise, it was a jack of hearts.

"Wait, how did you know which card it would be without looking?" she asked. The chances of a random card turning out to be a jack seemed pretty slim. Silvana must have either peeked or gotten lucky.

Silvana's eyebrows furrowed together. "He pointed," she explained.

Anna Luiza's heart beat a little faster. "How did *he* know without looking?"

Silvana rolled her eyes. "He did look. Duh. Not everything works the way you think it does, just because you're older," she said.

Anna Luiza pressed her lips together. They kept playing. Somehow, Brucie won the game.

Anna Luiza was impressed. Last summer, it had been super obvious whenever Silvana was fibbing or hiding a secret, but her littlest cousin had grown up a lot in the past year. Go Fish didn't exactly require great skill, but this was a pretty complicated trick Silvana was pulling off. Anna Luiza had no idea how she was doing it. It was almost spooky.

Silvana didn't crack once on her straight-faced insistence that it was Brucie, not she, who was looking at his cards. If Anna Luiza were just a little more gullible, she might have been tempted to believe it.

That night, after bringing her grandparents more medicine and putting away the leftover pizza, Anna Luiza tucked Silvana into bed. "Will you read us a story?" Silvana asked.

"Us? Is Brucie sleeping here too?" Anna Luiza teased.

"No, of course not. He's just here for the bedtime story." Silvana held up the book she'd chosen.

"Ah. Which room is his bed in?" Anna Luiza asked.

Silvana wrinkled her forehead. "It's not a room. It's just a place. He calls it his resting place."

Anna Luiza's skin tingled when she heard that. Silvana was too young to know the phrase *final resting place*, but her imagination had nearly conjured it. Little kid brains were so weird and fascinating.

Anna Luiza shook off the creepy feeling. Brucie was an imaginary friend, not a ghost. She'd spent lots of summers at her grandmothers' house. She would already know if it was haunted. Silvana's word choice was just a coincidence.

"Scooch over," she said, and climbed in next to her cousin to read.

The next morning, Nana was feeling a lot better, but Anna Luiza made the breakfast pancakes anyway. She added chocolate chips to hers and Silvana's, and made the ones for Nana and Vovó heart-shaped—or as close as she could manage with the drippy batter—and served her grandmothers breakfast in bed. "These are delicious," Vovó said. "What are your plans for the day?"

"We're going on a treasure hunt!" Silvana said.

"We are?" Anna Luiza said, at the same time Nana asked, "What kind of treasure?"

Silvana didn't answer either of them. "We need shovels. Brucie says the treasure is buried." She put her hands on her hips and glanced around, as if she expected to find shovels in her grandparents' bedroom.

"Sounds like an adventure. You know where the tools are kept?" Nana asked. Anna Luiza nodded and cleared the plates. Vovó's eyes were already half-shut. They needed to let the grandmothers sleep.

"Hey, maybe we should go to the playground instead," she suggested when the breakfast things were all put away. For some reason, she felt weird about going on a treasure hunt—or about going on one that was Brucie's idea. She wanted to spend time with her cousin, but she'd had enough of her imaginary friend.

Silvana shook her head. "Brucie says the playground's a bad idea. We have to find the treasure today."

Anna Luiza crossed her arms. "Why?"

"Because he says so!"

Anna Luiza struggled to stay patient. "Hey,

can Brucie go away and let just you and me play today? Big-little cousin time before the others get here? We can go on a treasure hunt with everyone tomorrow. That will be fun." The other cousins were supposed to arrive the next morning. Anna Luiza was more and more eager for them to get there.

Silvana stuck out her chin and shook her head. Anna Luiza recognized that stubborn expression—everyone in the family had it. When Silvana got this way, it was very hard to argue with her. "Today's the day for the treasure hunt," she said. "Brucie and I are going, with or without you. He can't be here tomorrow. He's only around for two days."

"*I'm* in charge while the grandmothers are sick," Anna Luiza reminded her. But Silvana only shrugged. Clearly that technicality didn't matter.

Anna Luiza sighed. "I'll get my sneakers," she said. Silvana squealed like she'd been promised a puppy.

They got two shovels from the barn and headed into the woods. Silvana led the way, chattering with Brucie the whole time. Anna Luiza tuned her out. At least she only had to indulge this for one more day. Hearing that Brucie's stay had an end date had lifted her spirits considerably.

Just when Anna Luiza started wondering if her cousin might get them lost, Silvana stopped walking. "This is the spot," she announced. "Brucie says we should dig here."

Anna Luiza lifted the heavy metal shovel off her shoulder and joined Silvana in digging. "How far do we have to go?" she asked after a few minutes. Digging a hole turned out to be hard work. The ground was packed solid, and though her cousin was surprisingly strong for a little kid, Anna Luiza still had to do most of it. She was already sweating.

"Deeper," Silvana said. "And wider too."

Anna Luiza sighed and kept digging.

"Wider," Silvana said. "Deeper." And finally, "Brucie says we're getting close."

Anna Luiza climbed out of the hole and leaned on her shovel to rest. She looked down at the pit they'd created. "It looks like a grave," she said, and immediately wished she hadn't.

"Brucie says keep going," Silvana said. Anna Luiza climbed back in just to stop her cousin from talking. She thrust her shovel into the dirt. It hit something solid with a clang.

Anna Luiza's eyes went huge. Was it possible there really was some kind of treasure in this stupid hole? "I hit something," she said.

"Let me see it!" Silvana cried. Anna Luiza moved out of the way to avoid being shoved over. Silvana dropped to her knees and dug with her hands. She pulled something out of the dirt and held it up for Anna Luiza to see. Anna Luiza almost fainted.

"No," she said. "No no no no no no no."

Silvana was holding a skull.

"Put that back," she said. "Don't touch it. That's a— We need to get help." She didn't want to scare her little cousin by saying the skull looked human, but it definitely for sure appeared that way.

"It's the treasure!" Silvana said, triumphant.

"That's not treasure," Anna Luiza said slowly.

"Brucie says there's more! There are more bones, just keep digging."

Anna Luiza shook her head and tried to keep her voice calm. "This is bad, Silvana. I'm getting scared. Will you please go back home with me? I don't want to be here anymore."

Silvana narrowed her eyes. "We can't go. Brucie wants us to stay."

"Silvana—"

"He wants you to join his collection. He

wants you to be his friend."

Anna Luiza's pulse took off like a race-horse. Every muscle in her body screamed for her to run, but she couldn't leave her little cousin there. Not alone. And not with Brucie.

"Listen to me," she pleaded. "Brucie is not your friend." But Silvana wasn't listening. She was climbing out of the hole and lifting the heavy shovel. "What are you . . . No!" Anna Luiza screamed as the shovel slammed down toward her head. She raised her arms just in time, taking the blow to her elbows instead. Pain jolted through her, almost as intense as her fear. "Stop!" she yelled.

"He wants to be your friend! His friends are what he treasures!" Silvana shrieked like a kid possessed. She lifted the shovel again.

Anna Luiza no longer doubted that Brucie was very real.

Her only doubt was whether she would make it out of the woods alive.

She lunged out of the way and Silvana's shovel hit the ground instead of bashing into her skull. Anna Luiza scrambled out of the hole. She didn't have time to think. She barely had time to act. But she had to do something or she would be buried in the grave she'd just dug.

Silvana screeched and whirled in a circle, her shovel flying in all directions. Anna Luiza lifted her own shovel to protect her face, and felt the thud of metal on metal as Silvana's flat blade crashed against hers. The force of the impact vibrated through her bones, and sent her little cousin flying backward. Anna Luiza braced herself for a second blow. Instead, she heard a shovel drop, and watched with horror as Silvana's limp body hit the ground.

"No!" Anna Luiza cried. She grabbed her cousin's wrist and exhaled with relief. Silvana was out cold, but she still had a pulse. She was alive. They were alive.

And Brucie would be gone tomorrow.

"Don't you dare come back," Anna Luiza said out loud. Even she was surprised how tough and strong she sounded. But she was in charge, and she meant it. "Don't you dare come near my family again."

She lifted Silvana in her arms, and carried her cousin home.

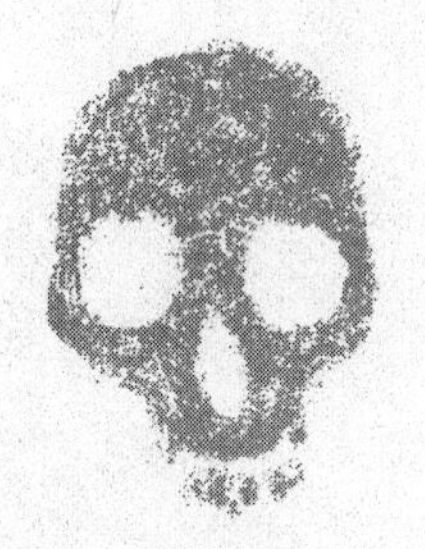

SUPERSTITION: THE PLAY

Author's note: The following play was performed by students at Blue River Elementary School on October 30 at the school's annual Talent Night. The performance came only a month after the mysterious disappearance of Assistant Principal Calvin Dunton, which left the town of Blue River shaken. There was talk among school administrators of canceling Blue River Talent Night, or changing its theme of "Superstition," but in the end it was decided, for the sake of morale, that the show must go on.

The adults involved have regretted that choice ever since, and many accusatory fingers have been pointed—but no assignment of blame could fix or change the tragic outcome.

In the weeks leading up to the sold-out performance, students rehearsed the play in secret, allowing no adults into the room. How much of what the audience witnessed was planned, I cannot say, for no trace of the original script was found—and, regretfully, no cast members remain.

What you are about to read has been pieced together from the memories of audience members who dared to relive the disturbing event. I record it here in order to preserve and honor the memory of those who were lost, but also to stand witness and serve warning.

Do not ever, *ever* read this script aloud, lest the terrible fate that befell its original performers should also descend upon you.

ACT I

The curtains part, revealing a nearly empty stage with only a park bench on it. TAWANA *enters from stage left, and* JACEY *from stage right. They walk toward each other, and stop in front of the bench.*

TAWANA: Hey, Jacey.

JACEY: Hey, Tawana.

TAWANA: Are you going to Abigail's sleepover tonight?

JACEY: I don't know. I want to, but I have to convince my mom. She doesn't want me leaving the house.

TAWANA: Why not?

JACEY: Isn't it obvious? Because of what happened to that kid in Silver Hill. Your parents aren't freaked out?

TAWANA: I mean, sure. Of course they are, but not so bad I can't go to a friend's sleepover. Tell your mom Abigail's parents will be home. Tell her we won't leave the house and there's safety in numbers. It's not like we'll be wandering the woods, hunting ghosts like that kid did.

JACEY: I told her. She's still worried. (JACEY *sits on the park bench.* TAWANA *joins her*) I heard her talking on the phone with my aunt. They think the Vanisher is back.

TAWANA: The Vanisher?

JACEY: Yeah, you know—the one who makes little kids disappear into thin air. Poof! Vaporized.

TAWANA: (*shaking her head*) This town is too superstitious.

JACEY: Well, my mom is, for sure. But . . . you don't believe in the Vanisher?

TAWANA: Are you kidding? Of course I do. That's why I would never summon it.

JACEY: (*stunned*) Summon it? What do you mean?

TAWANA: (*stands quickly*) Uh, nothing. Forget I said that.

JACEY: No, tell me!

TAWANA: I've gotta go. (*walks offstage, calling over her shoulder*) Talk to your mom! You should be there!

JACEY: (*to herself*) Well, that was weird. (*stands up*) I guess I'll go talk to my mom.

ACT II

The curtains part, revealing ABIGAIL, TAWANA, MABEL, *and* SYLAS *sitting on a floor spread with sleeping bags. Each of them holds a flashlight under their chin. Behind them, a full moon shines through the window, through which one also sees the silhouetted branches of a leafless tree.*

MABEL: (*in a ghostly voice*) Oooooooooh. (ABIGAIL *swats her arm, and all four friends collapse into giggles*)

ABIGAIL: (*catching her breath*) You are too much.

MABEL: (*shrugs*) You're the one who dared me to.

SYLAS: Mabel, it's your turn to ask.

MABEL: (*sits up straight*) Okay, Sylas. Truth or dare?

SYLAS: Dare!

MABEL: Hmmm. I dare you to . . . howl out the window like a werewolf. (SYLAS *jumps up*)

TAWANA: (*teasing*) How do you know he isn't a werewolf?

MABEL: Ha, I guess we'll find out.

SYLAS: (*opens the window and sticks his head out*) Arrrr-roooooo! Arrr-roooooo! (MABEL, ABIGAIL, *and* TAWANA *laugh*) Arrr-AAAAAAHHHHHH! (*his howl turns into a scream*)

ABIGAIL: What? What happened?

SYLAS: (*slams the window shut*) Oh my gosh. Oh my gosh. Oh my gosh. Oh my gosh.

TAWANA, ABIGAIL, and MABEL: What?

SYLAS: I saw something.

MABEL: Sylas, you're scaring me. This better not be a bad joke.

TAWANA: What did you see?

SYLAS: I saw— (*A knock comes from the window.* SYLAS, ABIGAIL, MABEL, *and* TAWANA *all scream and clutch one another. The knock sounds again*)

ABIGAIL: (*whispering*) What should we do?

TAWANA: (*hides her eyes*) I can't look.

MABEL: I can't look away! (A *face appears in the window.* MABEL *shrieks, then her shriek turns into laughter*) It's—it's Jacey!

TAWANA, ABIGAIL, and SYLAS: Jacey! (MABEL *opens the window.* JACEY *climbs through it, into the room*)

TAWANA: Oh my gosh, you scared us.

JACEY: Sorry! I had to sneak out. My mom wouldn't let me come.

ABIGAIL: Yeah, but you didn't have to sneak in. My parents know you're invited.

JACEY: (*sheepishly*) Oh. Good point.

MABEL: (*laughing*) That was epic. We almost died from fright.

JACEY: How do you think I felt when I heard Sylas howling like a werewolf?

SYLAS: I was pretty good, wasn't I?

JACEY: You almost fooled me.

TAWANA: We're glad you're here. You're just in time for truth or dare.

JACEY: Oooooh. (JACEY *takes off her backpack and unrolls her sleeping bag.* JACEY, SYLAS, MABEL, TAWANA, *and* ABIGAIL *settle onto the floor*)

ABIGAIL: Where were we? Oh, right—it's Sy's turn to go.

SYLAS: Jacey. Truth or dare?

ACT III

The curtains part, revealing ABIGAIL, SYLAS, TAWANA, JACEY, *and* MABEL *lined up in their sleeping bags. The room is lit only by moonlight.* ABIGAIL *snores, softly at first, then with a loud snort that makes* SYLAS *and* MABEL *giggle.*

ABIGAIL: (*woken up by the giggles*) Huh? Oh. (*She rolls over and goes back to sleep. After a moment,* JACEY *sits up and looks around*)

JACEY: (*softly*) Tawana. (*Pause. She nudges* TAWANA *gently.* TAWANA *doesn't move*) Tawana?

TAWANA: Mph.

JACEY: Are you awake?

TAWANA: I am now.

JACEY: Sorry. (*pause*)

TAWANA: What?

JACEY: What?

TAWANA: (*sits up*) What did you wake me up for?

JACEY: Oh. Nothing. I mean . . . never mind. (MABEL *and* SYLAS *sit up too*)

MABEL: You might as well say it, whatever it is, since now we're all awake. (ABIGAIL *snores loudly*) Okay, not all of us.

SYLAS: I couldn't sleep, either. I keep closing my eyes and thinking I see the Vanisher. That's what I thought you were,

Jacey, when I saw you climbing up that tree. The Vanisher coming to get us.

TAWANA: You can't see the Vanisher.

SYLAS: You can't?

TAWANA: No. And it can't just come get you. You'd have to summon it.

MABEL: I've heard that too. But it's funny to think of it climbing up trees.

JACEY: (*to* TAWANA) That's what I wanted to ask, actually. What you meant before about summoning it.

TAWANA: You woke me up to ask how to summon the Vanisher? No way. Let's go to sleep.

MABEL: If you know, you have to tell us.

TAWANA: Why?

SYLAS: Because we need to know. Knowledge is power.

TAWANA: Not in this case it's not. Believe me, you are all better off staying in the dark.

MABEL: I thought the dark is when ghosts and monsters and vampires come out.

TAWANA: Well, lucky for you, I don't know how to summon any of those.

SYLAS: If you don't tell us how to do it, one of us might summon it by accident. That's what my cousin thinks happened to that Silver Hill kid. He summoned the Vanisher without even knowing he'd done it, and: poof. Gone.

ABIGAIL: (*sits up without any of the others noticing*) Hey. (SYLAS, MABEL, TAWANA, *and* JACEY *jump*) Oops. What are you guys doing?

MABEL: Summoning the Vanisher.

ABIGAIL: Haha. You don't believe in that thing, do you?

TAWANA and JACEY: Yes.

SYLAS and MABEL: No.

SYLAS: I mean, maybe. You don't?

ABIGAIL: No way. My sisters did the thing

you do to summon it and it totally didn't work.

TAWANA: Maybe they did it wrong.

ABIGAIL: Or maybe it's fake—just a story kids tell to scare each other. Do you believe in the boogeyman too? (TAWANA *looks away and doesn't answer)*

SYLAS: If it's not real, show us.

ABIGAIL: Show you what?

MABEL: How to summon it! Let's do it together.

ABIGAIL: Now?

JACEY: I don't think—

SYLAS: (*cutting her off*) Yeah, let's try it!

MABEL: Come on, it'll be fun!

ABIGAIL: (*shrugs*) Sure, I'll show you. I'm not chicken. (*She stands up.* MABEL *and* SYLAS *stand too)*

MABEL: (*pumps her arms like chicken wings, looking down at* TAWANA *and* JACEY) Bawk bawk! (JACEY *stands up slowly)*

TAWANA: No way.

ABIGAIL: (*shrugs*) Fine. We'll do it without you.

JACEY: I'm not so sure this is a good idea. Even if it is just a story. Why take the chance?

MABEL: It's good to confront your fears. Face them head on! This will prove you've got nothing to be afraid of. I promise, it's just a fun game. (*she switches to an overly dramatic spooky voice*) Unless it's not. (JACEY *smiles and seems to relax*)

TAWANA: (*crosses her arms*) It's not a game to the Vanisher.

ABIGAIL: Whatever. Okay, Mabel, you stand there, and Sylas and Jacey, come over here. Good. Now, we're going to turn in circles like this. On each full spin, repeat these words: Vanisher, Vanisher, take me away. (*she spins and chants, saying the words quickly to get them out in a single spin*)

SYLAS: How many times?

ABIGAIL: Five.

TAWANA: (*quickly*) Only five. Make sure you stop at five.

ABIGAIL: (*ignores her*) Ready? (*she spins*) Vanisher, Vanisher, take me away. (*she stops*) Hey, aren't you going to do it with me?

ABIGAIL, SYLAS, MABEL, and JACEY: (*spinning, and chanting louder with each turn*) Vanisher, Vanisher, take me away. Vanisher, Vanisher, take me away. Vanisher, Vanisher, take me away. Vanisher, Vanisher, take me away.

TAWANA: (*jumps up*) No, stop, don't! (*she lunges toward* ABIGAIL) Stop! This is your seventh!

ABIGAIL, SYLAS, MABEL, and JACEY: Vanisher, Vanisher, take me away.

TAWANA: (*screams*) No! (*just as she reaches* ABIGAIL, ABIGAIL *disappears*) No! (SYLAS, MABEL, JACEY, *and* TAWANA *vanish as well*)

Author's note: With the sudden disappearance of the actors from the stage, stunned audience members waited for the kids to return. Eventually, a few people clapped, thinking the play must be over and the actors would come take their bows. But the event we'd just witnessed was not a trick of the light or part of the play. The children did not reappear.

A cry went up from the middle of the audience, as the first person realized the five students had truly vanished. Seemingly all at once, the rest of the audience caught on, and panic and chaos erupted.

I will not attempt to recount the minutes and hours that followed, as the deep distress and confusion of every person present made us all unreliable witnesses. Even my own memories of the course of events I do not fully trust.

But all this time later, two facts remain: The play was over. And the children who summoned the Vanisher were never seen again.

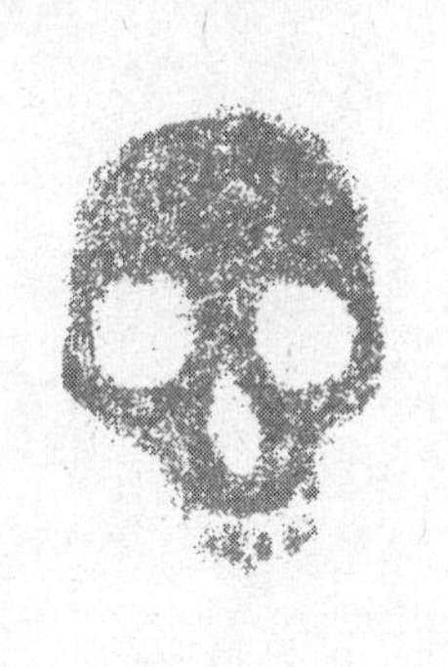

THE BOY AND THE CROW

The boy had never really thought about the crow before. He knew it existed, of course, but he rarely had reason to notice. It didn't affect him. It was just *there*. It was weird of his friend to be pointing it out.

If you looked around, the crows were everywhere. Lots of people had one. It's just the way things were.

"You know what a group of crows is called? A *murder*," the friend said.

The boy smiled. The crows were harmless.

In fact, in some ways, they were good.

The crow dropped a cookie on the boy's lunch tray. "You've earned it," the crow said, and flew a short distance away.

The boy picked up the cookie. It was chocolate chip and still warm from the oven. It smelled delicious.

"What did you do to earn it?" the friend asked between bites of an apple.

The boy knew the answer. The crow had mentioned it once before. "I work hard," he said.

"You do," the friend agreed. "So do I."

The boy shrugged. "I guess the crow thinks I work harder."

"Hmm," the friend said.

The boy felt bad for a second. The crow had never brought the friend a cookie. But the boy often shared his, so the crow was good for the friend too. Besides, the boy hadn't asked to be rewarded.

He broke the cookie in two and held out the smaller half. The friend accepted. They both chewed. The boy felt pleased with his generosity.

"You never wonder about it? Where they came from? Why they're like this? What it would be like if we shooed them away?" the friend asked.

The boy shook his head. "Why would I?"

The friend's eyebrows jumped. The boy quickly explained: "It's like gravity. You can't change it, so what's the point in thinking about it? You don't think about the air all day, do you?"

"I do if someone stinks it up with a fart," the friend said.

The boy snorted. The crow snickered. The bell rang, and lunch was over.

After school, the boy walked home with his sister, like usual. The crow swooped along beside them. It was annoying, suddenly being so aware of its presence. The boy kept noticing small things, like that his sister didn't have one. Like how sometimes the crow tossed pebbles in her path. Like how sometimes it cleared them from his.

What was the big deal? Pebbles didn't matter. The crow didn't matter. The friend was getting worked up about nothing. The boy felt huffy just thinking about it. He whirled around to check what the crow was doing—*nothing. See?*—and when he turned back, he walked straight into a tree.

"Ow!" the boy cried. His hand flew to his nose, which smarted from the impact. Tears prickled his eyes. He felt humiliated as much as hurt.

"Are you okay?" the sister asked. The boy shook her off and kept walking. He didn't want her—or the crow—seeing his tears.

But he knew from the cackle behind him it was too late.

The crow landed on the boy's shoulder. The boy stiffened. "Awww," the crow said softly, right into the boy's ear. The boy relaxed for a second, thinking the crow was comforting him. But it pecked his skin, hard, where a tear had escaped down his cheek. "You baby," the crow hissed. "Weakling."

The boy walked faster. He wanted to scream and push the crow away. He wanted to let all the tears he'd been holding in fall. But he didn't.

The boy wiped his cheek, smearing it with blood. "Ha," he said in his toughest voice. "Whatever."

The sister ran to catch up. "Hey. Are you all right?" she said.

The boy couldn't box up his feelings any longer. He picked up a pebble and flung it at his sister—not hard enough to hurt her, just hard enough to sting. It bounced off her arm. She stared at him in shock.

"Are you all right?" he mimicked in a squeaky, horrible voice. The sister shrank, and the boy felt a surge of power. On his shoulder, the crow chortled.

The sister stormed off down the sidewalk, and the boy laughed. The crow laughed too. Other crows around them joined in. The boy didn't feel quite so lousy anymore. He looked down at his forearms, where dark, soft feathers grew. They were beautiful, just like the crow's.

The boy walked home proudly.

That night after dinner, he took a stroll with his dad around the neighborhood. The crow came too, along with the dad's crow—sometimes hopping, sometimes flying, but not really *with* them. Just there.

The boy lowered his voice. "Do you ever think about the crows?" he asked.

The dad shrugged. "Not really. What is there to think about?"

The boy was pleased. "That's what I said!" he said. "My friend who doesn't have one was weird about it today. Saying, like, maybe we should shoo them off and turn down the things they give us. That maybe it isn't fair."

The dad rolled his eyes. "You're supposed to give up your crow just because not everyone has one? What would that solve?"

The boy had no answer, but the dad didn't expect one.

"Look," the dad said. "This friend. The one looking for handouts. Being sensitive. Always bringing up crows. Don't listen! It's all nonsense. The system works for us. Always has. And the only thing wrong with it is people like the friend, who want to change it. Eat your cookies, son. Enjoy what you've earned. You deserve it."

The boy beamed. The crows cooed. The dad was right. Of course he was.

They turned the corner and saw a

commotion. Across the street, a stranger ducked for cover as five, six, seven crows swooped down to attack, pecking and beating the stranger with their wings.

The boy's heart raced. "Should we help?" he asked.

The dad looked away. "Nah, I'm sure the crows have got it."

"Oh," the boy said, feeling foolish. He'd meant should they help the stranger. But of course if the crows were acting that way, the stranger had done something wrong. The crows had never attacked the boy like that, and he knew they never would. *He* wasn't the type to give them reason.

The boy walked on with his dad and ignored the kerfuffle. "Your feathers are really growing in nicely," the dad said.

The boy stood taller. "Thanks."

Over the next several weeks, the boy took the dad's advice and stopped thinking about the crow. If the friend brought it up, the boy changed the subject or stopped listening.

When the boy earned a cookie, he enjoyed it—sometimes sharing, sometimes not. He didn't want the friend to *expect* it.

The boy started spending less time with the friend and more time with the others in his class who had crows—but that was by coincidence, not design. The new friends were easy to talk to. They never, ever brought up the crows. They certainly never judged the boy for having one. And when the boy shared his cookies, these friends shared the candies, cupcakes, and chocolates their crows had brought them. The system worked well for everyone. Everyone who'd earned a crow.

One day, the boy bought his lunch and walked past the spot where he used to sit with the friend, way back when they had lunch together. He didn't even glance in the friend's direction, until he heard a noise that made him look—almost a squawk, but more like a sob.

The boy's gut twisted when he realized what was happening: The friend had cried out because of a crow—a crow that flew inches from the friend's face, taunting and teasing and mocking, until the friend broke down in tears. The boy couldn't hear what the crow was saying, but he didn't need to. He still saw what the friend was feeling.

"No!" the boy said without thinking. "Stop!" He slammed down his lunch tray and swatted the crow, shooing it away from the friend. "Enough!" he said, and the crow went still. It blinked at the boy. Other crows circled around them and tittered.

The boy was about to scold them too, when he realized what they were staring at: A dozen black feathers slid from the boy's arms and wafted to the floor. They formed a small pile at his feet.

He was losing them. He was losing his beautiful feathers.

Frantic, the boy looked at the fallen feathers, looked at the crows, and looked at the frightened yet grateful eyes of the friend. "Thank you," the friend said. "Thank you for standing up for me."

The boy started to shake. Standing there in the circle of crows and seeing his feathers drop, he felt vulnerable. Powerless. Alone.

He finally saw the crows for what they were. He finally got what there was to lose.

The boy stared at the friend. The friend stared back.

"Caw!" a crow said.

"Caw!" the crows answered, and the boy understood what was about to happen.

The crows lifted their beaks and prepared to attack. The air filled with the sound of their wings.

The boy closed his eyes against it. He did

not warn the friend. It soon was too late for warnings.

"Caw!" the crows cried as they swooped and pecked.

"Caw, caw!" the boy said, and ruffled his feathers.

It was time to join the murder.

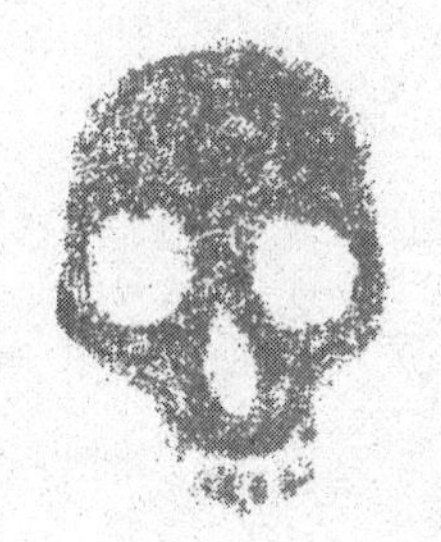

Two Wishes

Terry was reading on the couch with his softly snoring dog when his sister came home. She went upstairs without even stopping to take off her coat.

"Hey," Terry called.

"Hey, yourself," Trish replied, and closed the bedroom door behind her.

Terry sat up. *That's weird,* he thought. His book fell shut, but his finger marked his place. He looked at the dog. Bowser gazed back, heaved a doggy sigh, and let his eyelids droop shut.

Terry used the TV remote as a bookmark and stood. It wasn't like Trish to breeze past him. His twin-sibling radar detected something fishy, and Terry was instantly curious. Whatever Trish was up to, he wanted to know—especially if she was trying to keep it secret.

He tiptoed upstairs, avoiding the squeakiest step, and stood by Trish's door, holding his breath. He listened without moving but didn't hear a sound. He would have to go inside.

In one swift motion, Terry turned Trish's doorknob and pushed open the door, knocking once as he entered. "Hey, sis."

Trish swiveled in her desk chair, eyes wide with shock, then narrow with fury. "Excuse me. Don't you know how to knock?" she said.

Terry grinned. "I did knock," he said. Her face twisted with annoyance. Terry pretended not to notice the old, weathered notebook she clutched to her chest—the one she'd been reading when he entered—and kept talking.

"Just wanted to know if you'd like a snack. I'm about to make nachos."

Trish's shoulders relaxed but her grip on the notebook didn't. "No, thanks," she said. "Can you close the door? I'm trying to study."

"Sure," Terry said. "Good luck. Study hard." He backed out of the room without acknowledging the notebook. The best way to get his hands on it was to pretend he had no interest in it at all.

That night while Trish was taking a shower, Terry snuck down the hall to her room. He checked her usual hiding places—under the mattress, top shelf of the closet, back of the middle desk drawer—but didn't find the notebook. *Did she take it into the bathroom with her? Yeesh*, he thought, peeking inside her school binder. No notebook.

He was just about to give up when, in a flash of twintuition, he checked inside her pillowcase, and there it was.

He opened it quickly—Trish would finish her shower any second now—and read the beautiful, faded calligraphy that looped across the first page.

Rule One, it said. *One wish per person (no wishing for more wishes).*

It's a fairy tale, Terry thought. *But why hide that?*

Rule Two: No wish can undo another wish.

Wait, are these, like, instructions? he wondered.

Rule Three: The Wish Book must be found, not given.

Terry read the last line, intrigued.

Rule Four: Be careful what you wish for.

Ha. He turned the page.

Terry's heart sped up when he saw what came next: page after page of handwritten wishes, scrawled in many different languages, by all different hands. He flipped through the ancient, yellowed pages, being careful not to bend them, and read some of the wishes.

I wish we were rich.

i wish i could turn invisible.

I wish Father wasn't sick.

I WISH TO GET A GOOD PRICE FOR THE CALF.

I wish the hurricane never happened.

I wish Albertus loved me back.

I wish to die old and happy.

I wish to live forever.

A thrill shot up Terry's spine. Was this real? Real magic? Surely not, but the Wish Book was a cool idea even if it didn't make wishes come true. He wondered what his sister had written.

Terry turned to the last page of wishes, but saw only unfamiliar handwriting. Trish hadn't made her wish yet. He was dying to know what she'd choose.

With a start, he realized the shower water was off. He slipped the Wish Book into the pillowcase, tossed the pillow onto the bed, and dashed over to Trish's bookshelf, just as she entered the room. He pulled a random book from the shelf.

"Hey, sis," he said, trying not to sound guilty of snooping. "Sorry to be in your room, but is it okay if I borrow this?"

Trish straightened the towel on top of her head and lifted both eyebrows. "You want to borrow *The Girly Girl's Guide to Super Sleepovers*?" she said.

Whoops. Terry's cheeks flushed. He hoped she wouldn't notice. "Yeah," he said with a shrug. "I figured I might learn something, you know?"

Trish nodded. "You might. Let me know. I haven't read it."

Terry glanced at the sparkly cover. "Aunt Donna gift?" he said.

She smirked. "You guessed it."

"Cool. Well, thanks!" He bolted, sweating relief.

Every night for the rest of the week, Terry snuck into Trish's room and checked the Wish Book. Every night, he found it the same: no new wish from Trish.

It didn't surprise him, really. It was just like Trish to take her time, think things through, and make sure her wish wasn't wasted. She was the careful twin. Terry was the impulsive one.

He was tempted to grab a pen and write a wish of his own, but then he'd be caught, and of course she'd be furious. Besides, his wish kept changing. And what he really wanted, most of all, was to find out *hers*. This was better, even, than finding a secret diary, because he'd only have to read one sentence, and he was sure it would tell him everything.

On Saturday, Terry took Bowser to the park, where they played fetch and ran through puddles and snow. He was toweling Bowser off in the kitchen afterward when his mother appeared, looking distracted.

"Did Trish go with you?" Mom asked.

Bowser wagged his tail beneath the towel. "Nope," Terry said. He wiped the mud from

Bowser's hind paws.

"Well, have you seen her? Do you know where she is?" Mom pressed.

"Nope and nope," Terry said. Bowser wiggled free, grabbed a squeaky toy, and tossed it in the air.

"Hmm," Mom said. "It's not like her to go off without telling us. She didn't even leave a note. When she gets back, have her call me at Aunt Donna's, okay?"

"Sure," Terry said. Bowser tossed the toy again. Terry picked it up and threw it for him. "You know, if you got us cell phones, you'd be able to text her."

Mom rolled her eyes. "Nice try. Not until you're thirteen." She kissed him on the head and left.

As soon as the door closed, Terry ran up to Trish's room. Sure enough, she was gone—but the Wish Book was there, lying open on her desk. She hadn't even bothered to hide it.

Her favorite purple pen lay uncapped beside it. Wherever she had gone after writing her wish, it looked like she'd left in a hurry.

Terry stepped closer and read what his sister had written: I wish I could fly.

His heart skipped. *Seriously?*

He read it again and shook his head. *What a waste of a wish.* Humans couldn't fly. That impossible wish would never come true. Even if the Wish Book was magic, no way was the magic that strong. He couldn't believe Trish had done that.

No wonder she was gone.

Terry pictured his twin writing the words in her careful penmanship, realizing her wish was wasted, and fleeing the room in tears. She'd probably gone for a walk to burn off her disappointment. Terry almost felt sorry for her.

But . . . now that Trish had written her wish, maybe he could write one. He *had* just found the Wish Book, so it was fine according to the rules.

He sat in her chair and thought about what to wish for. A million dollars? A week of snow days? For Steve, Mom's boring boyfriend, to go away?

No, that would make Mom sad. Terry didn't want his wish to hurt anyone. And as Trish always said when Terry joked about breaking them up, their mom had a right to her own choices. Even dull choices. Even choices with coffee breath. *Ugh.* Maybe he'd wish for Steve to discover Tic Tacs. That would be nice for everyone.

Nah, a million dollars is better.

Terry picked up the pen and something buzzed past his ear. He yelped. The pen dropped.

An enormous bug with shimmering wings landed on top of the Wish Book. It looked straight at him. Terry stared back.

Trish would freak if she saw this bug in her room—she hated bugs, especially ones that flew—but Terry was entranced. The bug was beautiful. He'd never seen one like it. Its dark brown eyes, the same shade as his sister's, sparkled like jewels, and the purple in its wings matched the ink of the wish it stood on: I wish I could fly.

Wait.

Terry swallowed hard. "Trish?" he said to the bug, and immediately felt ridiculous. But when he said her name, the bug hopped as though it was excited. As though it was responding. Confirming.

Oh no. "Trish?" he said again. "Is that you?"

The bug lifted off the page and did a loop-de-loop through the air. Terry's heart sank to his toes. "Oh no," he said aloud. "Oh no oh no oh no."

The bug landed on his hand like it wanted to comfort him.

He sucked in a breath. "Oh, Trish. What have you done?" The bug fluttered its wings. Terry started to cry.

His sister was a bug. A beautiful bug! But a bug nonetheless.

Never again would she sneak into his room late at night so they could stay up whispering and giggling. Never again would she annoy him to death by humming the song from her favorite cartoon, or make him smile with a random fart joke, or break the last cookie in half to share. Never again would he trade his milk for her orange slices at school lunch, or check his answers against her perfect math homework, or catch her eye across the table as Steve told a long, boring story, knowing she knew exactly what he was thinking. Never again would she be his real sister, because somehow, impossibly, ridiculously, *horribly*, his sister was now a bug.

He couldn't stand it. Sometimes, sure,

Trish drove him up the wall, but life without her would be terrible. She was his twin. His other half. They were meant to go through the world together.

He had to fix this.

Terry knew the second rule: No wish can undo another wish. So he couldn't change her back. But there was another way for her to be his twin again.

Fingers shaking, Terry picked up the purple pen. He wrote the words quickly, before he could chicken out.

I wish to be a bug like this one.

The second he finished, it was done.

Terry didn't feel it happen, but he knew in an instant it had worked. Everything around him looked familiar yet completely different. Trish's room suddenly seemed enormous. He fluttered his wings (he had wings!) and felt them lift him off the chair. He could fly! This was amazing. He tried a loop-de-loop. His heart soared.

He was a bug now, just like his sister. It was a huge, unthinkable sacrifice, but it would be a fun adventure too.

"Hey, Trish!" he said, or rather, buzzed. He flew toward the other bug. "Trish!" he buzzed again. The bug hissed and flew off.

"Trish?" Terry repeated. She didn't answer.

What the huh?

Before Terry could wrap his bug brain around it, the front door slammed and someone ran up the stairs to his bedroom. "Terry!" he heard.

No. Impossible.

"Terry!" a voice just like his sister's shouted again. The footsteps pounded from his room to hers, and Trish appeared in the doorway—human Trish. Her hair looked windswept. Her eyes shone bright. Her face seemed bursting with news to tell him.

"Terry?" she said. But Terry knew she hadn't seen him. He glanced around and saw the other bug at the window, searching for a way out. Being a normal insect. Just like it had been all along.

Terry felt like he'd swallowed a bonfire.

He'd been wrong. So wrong. So above and beyond wrong—and so foolishly impulsive—he almost couldn't believe it.

But Trish would believe it.

Trish knew better than anyone what Terry was like.

She always said if he'd just *think* another second or two before he acted, she wouldn't constantly have to dig him out of trouble. But she did.

Trish always saved him. She would rescue him from this hideous mess. He only had to tell her what he'd done.

But how?

Trish moved toward the desk like she was

showing him the answer. And there it was: *The Wish Book!* He would land on his wish and she'd see it and him, and put two and two together. Then somehow she'd find a way to fix it.

He flew toward her and she shrieked. "It's okay," he said. "Trish, it's me." Though he knew she could not understand him.

He hoped he wasn't making a second enormous mistake.

He landed on the desk, on top of the Wish Book. On top of his wish. He fluttered his wings, held his breath, and silently begged his twin to get it. To understand him.

It's me, it's me, it's me, it's me, he thought, trying to throw the words where she might catch them. Hoping harder than he'd ever hoped before.

She blinked.

He watched her face transform into a familiar expression. Her eyes filled with calm. Her jaw tightened. He saw it and knew: Trish was forming a plan.

Yes, sis. Yes!

Slowly, she reached out and picked up the pen behind him. Her lips twitched with the start of a smile. His whole body beamed back joy.

She lifted her hand and he saw what she was holding.

The pen was still on the desk behind him.

Her trusty fly swatter was not.

Beware! If a bed monster nibbles your toe,
she won't leave the rest well alone.
She'll slide out your toenails, peel back the
    skin,
and suck your flesh clean off the bone.

When she reaches your ankle, she'll lick up
    the blood,
and take a good chomp of the meat.
That's why it is safest, everyone knows,
to keep blankets over your feet.

If the blanket slides off in the night, my
poor friend,
you can kiss foot and leg both goodbye.
The monster will gobble what bites she can
get.
She won't stop till she reaches your thigh.

But then it is not 'cause she's full that she'll
stop,
nor is it so that she can rest.
The monster will switch to your other bare
foot
and compare which of them's tasting best.

You can fight, you can scream, you can cry,
you can beg,
but the monster won't care, not a little.
For after she's eaten both legs, now she gets
to devour your soft, tasty middle.

The middle's the best and the squishiest
part—
plus it's full of the most nutrients.
Each organ she gnaws on she'll savor, not
giving
a darn if the sound makes you wince.

It's not because monsters are selfish or
cruel—
they're mostly quite charming and funny.
It's just that the children whose beds they
sleep under
can smell irresistibly yummy.

Where were we? Ah, yes—eating liver and
guts,
your intestines and kidneys and heart.
When the monster's slurped up all the best
of that mess
you'll be looking quite well torn apart.

There's nothing at this point to do, I'm
afraid.
Your loss is the monster's true gain.
For after she's finished your lungs and
your neck,
she gets to move on to your brain.

She'll pluck out your eyes (mmm, they're
salty and juicy),
and save all your nose hairs for later.
Once she has eaten your face off, your ears
will border two sides of a crater.

She'll pry back the top of your skull like
the lid
from a can of baked beans, only better—
for inside your head there's a smart, chewy
treat:
It's like beef mixed with cheese, only
wetter.

She'll munch it and crunch it and chew all
that's left,
and let out a terrible belch.
If, in her belly, you try to protest,
your last cries the bed monster will squelch.

Not a gulp or a bite will be left of you, see,
she'll have eaten you, toenail to head.
And once she has polished off every last
drop,
she'll curl up and she'll sleep in your bed.

I would hate for this fate to befall one of
you,
my delicious and innocent children.
So turn off the lights, and aim for sweet
dreams—
but please, keep your toes tucked and
hidden.

ACKNOWLEDGMENTS

Howls of thanks to my editor, Rosemary Brosnan, who helps me find my way through the deepest, darkest forests. A grateful shudder to the entire team at Quill Tree Books and HarperCollins, especially Courtney Stevenson, David DeWitt, Caitlin Lonning, and the monstrously talented marketing, sales, publicity, and subrights ghouls. Carolina Godina, your illustrations are so perfect, I screamed.

Thanks to my agent, Michael Bourret, for keeping me safe while I dream. A thunderclap for everyone at Dystel, Goderich & Bourret.

Bone-deep hugs to Lainie Fefferman, Jascha Narveson, Jem Altieri, David Levithan, Billy Merrell, Nick Eliopulos, Jeff Snyder, Anna Luiza Rissi, Sophia Jane Rissi,

Erika Rissi, Jeremy Rissi, Mama Mrose Rissi, and Ati Rissi, who listened to early drafts and didn't mind the cobwebs. Chris Crew, Claire Legrand, Emily X.R. Pan, Lauren Strasnick, Robin Wasserman, Erin Soderberg Downing, Terry J. Benton, Terra Elan McVoy, Tiff Liao, and Amy Jo Burns helped the moonlight sneak through the clouds.

Scritches to Arugula Badidea, my very ferocious ostrich, for staying right there in the middle.

A tingle up the spine to Alison Johnson, Island Readers & Writers, and the librarians, educators, and booksellers who help readers find books to devour—especially those at Labyrinth Books, Community Bookstore, McNally Jackson Books, Princeton Public Library, and Stonington Public Library, who keep this book monster well fed.

And a whisper of thanks to you, reader.